Shatter *Me*

Tori St. Claire

Entangled Publishing, LLC
2614 South Timberline Road
Suite 109
Fort Collins, CO 80525
Visit our website at www.entangledpublishing.com.

Brazen is an imprint of Entangled Publishing, LLC. For more information on our titles, visit www.brazenbooks.com.

Edited by Robin Haseltine
Cover design by Heather Howland
Cover art by Shutterstock

Manufactured in the United States of America

First Edition April 2105

To Sara L., because strength is beauty.

Chapter One

Promises sucked.

Especially when the promise had been made to a dying man.

Alex McCray tightened his grip on the steering wheel as he entered the city limits of Colton, Illinois. He fought down the threatening memory of chaos, explosions, bullets, and his best friend Drew Sanders's raspy voice. The nightmare haunted him every waking moment as it was, but being in Drew's hometown only made it more real. More inescapable. Eight months ago, he and Drew had planned to throw a barbecue when they returned home. But that inevitable day beyond the wire, just before the end of their last tour, changed everything. Now Alex was honor-bound to ensure Drew's widow was coping okay. Just what he wanted—to nurse Reagan's heartache when he couldn't get over his own.

He rolled past the first intersection and thumped a fist on the console between the seats. Reagan would want to know what happened. Want to know if Drew had suffered. Hell yes, he'd suffered. Drew had jumped on a live grenade and lost the lower half of his body. Worse, he'd done so to save Alex. No way could he tell her that he was responsible for killing her husband.

"Son of a bitch," Alex muttered. He sucked in a deep breath and gritted his teeth. *Just check on her. She'll be fine, all things considered. Then you're out of here.*

Free to go back to Chicago, kick back with his family at his surprise birthday party he wasn't supposed to know about, and start his life over as a project manager in his brother's engineering firm. Or maybe he'd accept a position as a civilian instructor at Scott Air Force Base. Though he didn't really care for that option; it made forgetting impossible.

Either way, he wouldn't be here, checking in on a woman he'd been more attracted to than he should have been, who'd put her husband in the ground less than a year ago.

But Drew's final words had been a request to look after Reagan, and Alex owed the man who'd saved his life that much. At least.

He turned a corner, taking the road that went past the school where Reagan taught third grade. The last time he'd been here, Drew had been driving. He'd stopped to surprise her at lunch, dragging Alex along with him. She'd made the entire lunchroom applaud their local heroes, much to his discomfort.

Drew had been so overjoyed to see her. She, on the other hand...she'd seemed happy, but distant.

An invisible fist wrapped around his gut. Oh hell, could Drew have read into things wrong, suspected Alex's interest? Nothing had ever happened between Alex and Reagan, but there had been one strange night that haunted Alex. They'd literally bumped into each other in the hallway while the neighbors, and Drew, were on the patio. Both of them had been drinking, but the look in her sky-blue eyes when he grabbed her by the elbow to keep her from falling and held on a moment too long... She'd walked away, as had he, but *something* lay behind her eyes. Something that grabbed him deep inside and twisted each time he tried to reason it out.

He ground his teeth together again. He didn't want to be here. He'd put off his promise for the first month of being home. Drew was the hero. He deserved a hero's memory. And Alex didn't intend to fuck it up any more, much less be constantly reminded of how he'd sent his best friend to the grave.

Ten minutes. Maybe fifteen. Then you're home free.

After all, this was just a quick check. Drew's life insurance certainly would have seen Reagan comfortable, and she had the means of supporting herself as well. This was nothing more than an obligatory condolence call.

He nosed around another turn, onto the quaint suburban street he'd been down a dozen times with Drew. Scraggly tree branches scattered across the first few yards. Bits of shingles littered lawns, and as he squinted to look beyond the immediate houses, evidence of more storm damage became clear. Gotta love the Midwest and its powerful storms. The round that had hit Chicago and knocked out several thousand people's power at the end of May must have barreled through here as well.

Good thing no one seemed to have suffered severe damage. Or if they had, they'd evidently cleaned it up, leaving only a little debris behind.

Except for the three-foot-wide hulking half of a tree across Reagan's smashed front porch.

And the bare spot on her roof where a two-foot-square patch of shingles had been sheared off.

And the faux shutter on her front window hanging on by its bottommost hinge.

Alex blinked. What the hell? Was that duct tape over the glass on the window?

He braked at the edge of her drive and glanced around, questioning whether he had the right house. It looked... abandoned. Certainly neglected. Had she moved? She must have. Evidence of repairs on her neighbor's roof stood out as he looked more closely—new shingles shone against the weathered gray shake. Orange stickers on the windows across the street marked three new replacements. And the house he'd passed, just to Reagan's east, was undergoing a new paint job.

Her car sat in the drive—no, she hadn't moved. So why was her house the only one on the block still in disrepair? That massive storm had come through three weeks ago.

He pulled in, eyeing the porch, debating whether it would fall on his head if he attempted the three steps to her door.

· · ·

At the sound of a car engine shutting off, Reagan marched toward the front door. Freaking contractors—this one was getting a piece of her mind. The first had taken her deposit and failed to show then avoided all her attempts to track him down via phone. The second showed up drunk and nearly hacked off his own leg when he put the chainsaw to the giant maple across her porch. He'd barely scarred the bark before she'd kicked him off the job. This would be the third, and he should have arrived four hours ago. Drew had left her in this damn bind. If he hadn't locked up his bank accounts, she might have been able to afford the deductible on a quality repairman, not some second-rate storm chaser. Then again, she shouldn't be surprised Drew found a way to control her, even from beyond the grave.

She jerked the door open, prepared to rip the roofer a new asshole. But what greeted her on her doorstep had her snapping her mouth shut and stepping back in stunned surprise. Alex McCray stood with his hand raised to knock, looking equally surprised.

Alex.

It took a minute for her brain to connect the pieces and send words to her mouth. She swallowed her surprise and smiled. "Alex? What are you doing here?"

No sooner had the question left her mouth than a flutter stirred in her belly that she experienced every time his deep forest green eyes connected with hers. God, eighteen months had passed since she'd last seen him, but he hadn't changed. The dark hair he kept just a little too long for regulation invited her fingers to slide through the hint of waves. His broad shoulders and muscular chest offered a safe haven she yearned to sail into. And the ever-present hint of stubble on his chin left her wondering how it would feel against her lips.

He smelled good, too. Spice and sweetness, completely unlike Drew's overpowering musk.

"Reagan? What the hell happened?" Concern bunched

his forehead and created crinkles at the corners of his eyes.

"Um." It took another second for her to collect her thoughts enough to realize he was talking about her damaged front porch. "Oh. Storm damage."

"I get that, but…" He trailed off with an arched brow.

"Hello to you, too, by the way." She stepped back from the door and beckoned him to enter. At least inside he was less likely to have the roof come crashing down on his head. No way was she telling him the whole sordid mess—she didn't want his pity. Not to mention, Alex would never believe the man who'd saved his life had left her in this predicament, much less accept the dark side of his best friend's personality. She waved her hand, dismissing the situation. "Stupid roofer hasn't shown up. I hired him…a while ago."

Alex's other eyebrow shot up to join the first. In the silence that stretched between them, she became acutely aware of how he filled up the living room. Her nerves tightened her stomach into knots. Her palms turned clammy, and her pulse skipped erratically. He made her giddy like a naive teenager all over again. And she was certainly far from naive.

She crossed her arms over her breasts to keep her hands still. "What are you doing here, Alex?" They'd talked once since he returned, since Drew had died. The phone conversation had been awkward at best. In a hundred years, she'd never dreamed he would show up on her doorstep, when she was finally able to acknowledge there was something unforgettable about him, and yet, she still couldn't. A ghost remained between them. One he viewed as a hero. One she knew was anything but.

"I, ah, wanted to see how you were doing." He glanced

at her, then quickly looked at the mantel. "How you were holding up."

Great. What exactly could she say? *I'm better off with him gone, now go away?* He'd never understand. Even if he could, she didn't want to be the one to tarnish Alex's memory of Drew. Alex was alive because of him. And in their short phone conversation, she'd gathered he didn't feel deserving. If he only knew the things she knew.

"You thought I'd want what?" *Furious color rose to his cheeks. His hand whipped out, the flat of his palm in a direct line with her cheek. "Did I ask you to think for me?"*

Reagan shoved aside the memory of Drew's last homecoming. She'd moved beyond the fear, and she wouldn't revisit it now. She cleared her voice and dropped onto the edge of the couch. "I'm doing okay. You?"

Pain flashed across his face before he smothered it with a tight smile. "Hanging in there, I guess. One day at a time. It's still weird sometimes. I keep expecting…" He frowned. "You know how it is."

Nope. She didn't. She knew freedom, and there wasn't a part of her that missed the fists, the yelling, the fear, and the absolute control Drew wielded over her life, including locking down their finances and making it virtually impossible for her to escape. Still, she nodded anyway.

As if he were afraid he might break it, Alex lowered himself gently into the sofa beside her. His thigh brushed hers. "What's the deal with the roofer?"

"Um." Heat crept into her cheeks. There was nothing more embarrassing than having to explain—to a stranger or even her best friend—how Drew had left his sister as his beneficiary because he'd never trusted her with a dime of his money. "Well, I was preoccupied with the end of school," she lied. No way was she going to open that can of worms. "I thought I hired someone legit. He took my money and ran."

Alex's frown deepened. "What about insurance?"

"Oh, it's covered by the policy. It's the deductible I have to meet." Five thousand dollars she'd had to scrape together the first time and certainly didn't have now. "When the first guy didn't show, I got smarter and refused to pay a deposit. Number two showed up drunk, so I fired him. Number three...well...he was supposed to be here at eight."

A tic pulled at the side of his jaw. "You're shitting me, right?"

She shook her head. "Nope." There was no reason to mention she'd been forced to find a virtual handyman this time around. And Alex's cologne was doing fantastic things to her mind, making her think of how nice it would feel to settle into his side and forget all the headaches. She smoothed her hands on her shorts and rose from the sofa. "Can I get you something to drink?"

She drew in a steely breath as she made her way to the kitchen. Talk about ironic. For the last five years, she'd had to watch every step she made around Alex for fear Drew would retaliate if she laughed too hard or smiled too brightly. Now, when she'd finally escaped her prison of a marriage, she still had to maintain the guise. All things considered, it would be easier if he left. Quickly.

Ignoring her question, Alex followed her and asked, "You think this guy will show up?"

Hardly. She opened the refrigerator and bent to peer inside. "Who knows. Beer?"

"Sure."

She grabbed two bottles, shut the door, straightened, and turned to pass him his beer, catching him staring at her ass. His gaze jerked to hers. For a moment, a spark of attraction flared between them. He quickly looked to the sliding glass door to her back patio as he accepted the drink from her shaking hand.

Oh, God. She closed her eyes for a half second and drew in a deep breath. Yeah. He needed to go. Before she did something she'd regret. Like touch him.

She popped the cap off her beer and took a long swig.

Alex gestured with his drink toward the backyard. "Desi and Chance know anyone who can fix the porch?" he asked of her neighbors, whom he'd met on several occasions. "And is it just me, or is it hot in here?" He tugged at the collar of his T-shirt.

"I don't have the air-conditioning on." Because the tree had taken it out as well—one compressor flattened like a pancake.

He threw her an *are you serious* look.

She shrugged. "Well, it's kinda toast, too."

"Jesus, Reagan," he muttered. "Can anything else go wrong at once?"

She couldn't help but chuckle. "Let's not tempt fate, shall we?"

At that, the deep lines on his forehead smoothed, and his mouth quirked with a half smile that made her heart stutter. Damn, he was more potent than she remembered. She gulped and fled to the safety of the living room, putting a good twenty feet of distance between them.

He didn't seem to take the hint. Following once more, he sat down beside her and reclined on the sofa, stretching long, muscular legs out in front of him. She told herself not to stare at the powerful thighs his jeans couldn't hide, but she couldn't help herself. Man, he was probably as beautiful naked as he was clothed. More so.

He cleared his throat, drawing her attention to his face. Heat rushed to her cheeks. Caught red-handed, staring. How embarrassing. Good thing he couldn't mind-read.

Then again, judging by the sudden intensity in his forest green gaze, maybe he could. She shifted sideways, far enough they weren't touching, but not so far away her attempt at distance would be overt.

"So, how long are you in town?" she asked. With any luck, he'd be gone within the hour. Because if he wasn't, she couldn't guarantee she could maintain the charade.

Chapter Two

Alex forced himself to look at Reagan's face and not her shapely legs. She'd always been pretty, always teased his mind, and he'd always been a bit jealous of Drew. But she'd never hit him this damn hard. Like a sucker punch in the face, she was right *there*. Knocking him off balance. Making it impossible to pretend he didn't see her. But now, the idea of checking out his best friend's widow felt even worse. Like he was disrespecting his friend's memory.

He steered his thoughts away from the satiny sheen of her skin and focused on the more immediate problem: Reagan was clearly in a bind.

He took a long, slow pull off his beer, mulling options. The honorable thing to do would be offer to help her out. He certainly owed Drew that much. But helping Reagan meant spending more time around the most fascinating woman he'd ever met. He wanted her like ice in the middle of a desert. Everything else aside, he didn't dare entertain that idea. She was recently widowed, and only a bastard took advantage of a woman's grief. Not to mention, he didn't even want to consider what she'd do when she found out he was responsible for her husband's death. She'd probably tell him to go straight to hell. Lord knew he wasn't a hero, deserving of her esteem.

Walking away, however, meant breaking his promise. Even more unacceptable. He still had his honor, and he refused to let it become any more tainted.

He leaned forward and set his beer on the coffee table. "How about I cut that tree off your roof, at least, before I take off?"

Reagan's eyes widened a fraction, then she gave him a nervous smile. "My contractor will probably show up tomorrow."

Right. Guys who wanted work didn't no-show. And evidently, she knew how to pick the rotten ones. Man, if Drew had been here, he'd have had the first guy's ass in a sling before he could skip town. Damn it. Why did Reagan have to be the one to suffer in his absence? She deserved better than being jerked around.

That sealed it—he was helping her out.

"Well, if he shows, he'll have that much less to do." Alex shrugged. He had four days before he had to be back for the party his sister was trying to pass off as a picnic. Saturday afternoon. Not that he intended to spend that much time with Reagan. Cutting down a tree would take a handful of hours, max. "I've got some time today. Might as well put it to use. That's what friends do, right? Help out friends."

At her furrowed brow, he hurried to add, "Drew would have wanted this."

Her frown deepened inexplicably, but she agreed with a terse nod. "Okay. I'll help you."

Like hell he'd let her climb up there and risk injury. All he needed was *that* on his conscience as well. "Nope, I've got it."

Reagan let out a heavy sigh. "At least let me take you to dinner, then."

Dinner with the one woman he should run far away from. An awkward dinner, no doubt, if their stilted conversation so far indicated anything. Hell, he didn't know what to say to her. Half of him wanted to apologize for Drew's death, and the other half of him wanted to grab her up and kiss her senseless.

"That's really not necessary."

"And it's not necessary for you to climb up on my roof and cut down a tree." Her smile was smug.

"Point taken." He grabbed his beer and downed the last of it. "All right then, dinner it is. I'll get to work. Tools are in the basement, right? Off the garage?"

She stood quickly and didn't look at him as she answered, "No, I moved them to the shed out back."

Damn, he'd never seen her so…uncomfortable. Normally, she laughed and teased. A wave of guilt washed over him. Here he was fighting to keep his hands off her, and she clearly still grieved. Hell, he was probably a reminder of Drew. God knew she brought back memories.

Alex sighed and pushed off the couch. "Listen, Reagan… if my being here makes you uncomfortable—"

"I'm good, really." She smiled the first genuine smile since he'd arrived, making her blue eyes twinkle with warm light.

"You sure? I know it's not easy — "

"It's fine." Her smile brightened, and she touched his elbow. "I just wasn't expecting all this."

Where her fingers rested against his skin, little currents of electricity sparked. He tensed against a razor-sharp surge of desire. Damn, he couldn't remember how long it had been since such an insignificant touch affected him so powerfully.

This is wrong. She belongs to Drew. She won't want you anyway once she learns what you did.

With that reminder, Alex jerked his arm away and hurried out the back porch door. He made a beeline for the work shed out back, a quaint little outbuilding that matched the house's sage green and white color. Expecting to have to navigate around the woodworking tools and sawdust-covered floor, Alex stopped abruptly in the doorway and stared in disbelief. Neat shelves now lined the walls with every tool Drew had kept in the basement sitting in its own space. The floor had been swept clean; not even a trace of sawdust remained. She'd set plants under false lighting down the length of the worktable. No hint lingered that this had ever been Drew's private sanctuary.

Odd. As close as Drew and Reagan had been, Alex would have assumed she'd leave a few things lying around as mementos. Lord knew Alex would have, if his wife had died. He wouldn't have been able to stand the thought of tearing apart her space.

And what was with moving the tools out here? What had she done in the basement, then?

He pushed the questions aside, determined to focus on the roof. What Reagan did was really none of his business. Everyone coped with grief in their own way. Maybe the reminders were too much to bear.

He grabbed the chainsaw, checked the gasoline and oil, and then hoisted the lightweight extension ladder onto his shoulder. Toting both across the lawn, he made his way between Reagan's house and Desi and Chance's to the tree that had been neatly split in half.

After assessing the best plan of attack, he decided to leave the upright portion of the tree to someone who knew more and to tackle what had broken off and smashed her front porch. He secured the ladder to the corner of the main wall and made his way up.

What he found when he set foot on the roof, however, only pissed him off. From the car, he'd assumed the missing shingles were just that—shingles sheared off from high winds. Up close, he found a different story. Not only were the shingles missing, but the damaged area was much larger than it looked from the driveway, and making matters worse, one section of plywood had been broken clean in half. If it rained, her front room would absolutely get wet.

"Son of a bitch," he muttered. Drew would never have let this happen, never let Reagan live like this. He'd have hired someone to take care of this immediately, even if it meant phoning from overseas.

The front door banged beneath him. Reagan walked across the front lawn to a small, recently planted sapling in the center of the yard. She dragged the hose from the opposite side of the house and dropped to all fours to work with the mulch around the sapling's trunk.

His gaze locked on her shapely thighs beneath her jeans shorts. The legs were cut just high enough that when she pushed back, he glimpsed the faintest hint of her ass. That sight was enough to make another part of his anatomy stand up and take notice.

Jesus, she'd fit into his hands perfectly. Hips just wide enough to make a man's mouth water. Strong legs. Trim little waist. Was she bare beneath those shorts, or did she indulge in sexy little panties? And if he knelt behind her, the way she pushed back as she moved…

He grimaced as his brain ran away with logic. Drew would spit nails if he knew what Alex wanted to do with that perfect bottom. This was wrong on so many levels—he had no business fantasizing about Reagan, no business thinking about anything but cutting down this tree. If he had any sense at all, he'd leave before he did something he couldn't take back.

But he'd given his word. He'd promised to make sure Reagan was doing okay. From all the evidence surrounding him, she was far from all right. Almost as if she was avoiding the truth of everything around her. No matter how much he wanted to run, he couldn't walk away.

Chapter Three

As twilight began to cast shadows throughout the neighborhood and cicadas struck their eerie song, Reagan's stomach growled. She rocked back onto her ankles, pulled off her gardening gloves, and appraised the flowers she'd planted around the base of her new tree. The dogwood had been a gift from Desi, a symbol of the new life she'd begun, and she'd given it the day Reagan's counselor told her he didn't think she needed his services any longer. She'd grown. Put the abuse behind her and no longer let it form her world. Sure, she'd carry the scars—not just the physical ones—but she'd healed. The rest she'd have to learn through living.

And this little sapling was her constant reminder that she'd never again be a victim. The flowers were just eye-catching, and their vibrant colors made her happy.

Her stomach growled again. Definitely time to eat.

Satisfied the flowers were appropriately planted, she stood and stretched and then turned to see how Alex was coming along. The chainsaw had stopped a few minutes ago, and as she scanned the roofline, she caught sight of his bare back. He faced the rear of the house, doing something with the roof she couldn't ascertain. But what she could see wreaked havoc on her mind.

He'd taken his shirt off at some point, and the fading sunlight cast a sheen over defined muscles that bunched and pulled as he moved. Mouthwatering—the man was the definition of eye candy.

As if he sensed her staring, he straightened and looked over his shoulder. The twist of his torso revealed a solid black tattoo that spanned his left bicep and shoulder. She couldn't make out the design from the distance, but that ink fascinated her. He was such a contrast to Drew, who wouldn't have inked his body if someone had held a gun to his head.

How many women had played with that tattoo? Traced it with their fingers? Explored it with their tongues? A vision of her doing just that gripped her so hard her womb contracted. Longing surged through her veins. God, what was the matter with her? He was so off-limits. Even if he wanted to acknowledge the attraction buzzing between them—and she was certain he wouldn't—she could never be herself around him. Could never share the truth of what Drew was really like outside his unit.

Besides, it wasn't as if she wanted to get involved on a deeper level. She'd found freedom, and she wouldn't be chained again.

She shoved all thought of exploring Alex's naked, sweaty body out of her mind and called up to him, "Are you hungry?"

He moved closer to the damaged edge and wiped his

forehead with the crook of his elbow. "Starved, but I'm a mess."

She chuckled. "I do have a shower."

A slow, teasing grin spread across his face. "Your water actually works?"

"Hah." With a middle-finger salute, she made her way to the rickety front porch. "Funny man. Come on, before I starve to death."

Taking care not to rip the door off its broken hinges, she entered her house and made for the kitchen to wash her hands. When she finished, Alex stood in the doorway between her living room and kitchen.

Up close and personal, he was even more of a sight to behold. His sun-bronzed body was hard and sculpted from collarbone to waistband. Her gaze followed the faint trail of dark hair that ran between firm pecs, down a washboard belly, only to disappear beneath the fly of his jeans. She tried desperately to stop herself from looking lower, but her willpower failed, and she dipped her gaze to the sizable bulge the denim couldn't fully hide. A shiver stole over her as yearning arced through her body. Eye candy, indeed. What she wouldn't give to explore by taste.

Suddenly aware of the path her thoughts had taken, she jerked her gaze back to his face.

Deep green eyes glinted so hot her breath caught and her throat went dry. She licked her lips, inadvertently drawing his attention to her mouth. His gaze remained fixed there, and in the heavy silence that enveloped them, his breathing hitched.

Or was it hers?

She couldn't tell. But before she melted into a puddle

right here in her kitchen, she needed to escape. With some-one else, she might have entertained the idea of a one-night hookup to get her back into the world of living. Yes, Alex McCray might be a walking sexual fantasy, he might even share her uncontrollable attraction, but he'd never betray Drew's memory by indulging in her.

"Shower's upstairs," she murmured.

Her words broke the spell that enveloped them. With a shake of his head, Alex cleared the heat from his gaze. "Shower sounds great, but these clothes…" He held out his balled-up, sweat-stained shirt. "Maybe we should stay in for dinner."

Oh, no. If they stayed in, she wouldn't be able to resist. Before she could stop her tongue, she'd spill all the reasons why it was okay for them to have sex. Starting with the fact that Drew had beaten the shit out of her more times than she could count, and he didn't deserve either Alex's or her loyalty.

Though maybe it wasn't necessary to confess if they were only talking one night of earth-moving orgasms.

No. It would never work. The ties that bound them ran too deep for a meaningless romp. Sex with Alex would be meaningful, even if she *wanted* it to be strictly physical. She'd desired him for too long. Harbored too many secret fantasies.

She glanced back at his handsome face, the damp dark hair sticking out at odd angles. His expectant look prodded her for an answer.

She inclined her head toward the shower upstairs. "Go ahead and clean up. I have some of Drew's old clothes around." One box remained, one she'd intended to send to

Goodwill at the end of the week. With a little luck, it wasn't full of winter clothes.

Alex answered with a nod and turned toward the stairs. "Towels still beneath the sink?"

"Yeah."

She waited until he reached the landing before she jogged to the basement for the box. Luck was in her corner, and the contents revealed shorts and shirts. Drew had been rangy, compared to Alex's stronger build, but they'd already confessed to sharing BDUs if one or the other had neglected laundry and needed a spare.

But the more Reagan looked at her former husband's clothes, the more an uneasy feeling swirled in her belly. She couldn't stand the idea of looking up from her dinner and seeing Drew sitting across from her. Didn't want to see Drew in Alex at all.

These would never suit.

She turned and bolted up the stairs, out the back door, and across the lawn to Desi's house. Reagan let herself inside the screened-in back porch and knocked on the living room entrance. *Please be home, please be home.* Chance was about the same height as Alex, and daily workouts at the gym gave him nearly the same build. Maybe not quite as broad across the shoulders, but it would do in a pinch. And this was definitely a pinch.

Desi answered with a perplexed frown. "Reagan? What's wrong?"

"Nothing's wrong." She glanced back at her house, aware of the ticking clock. "I need to borrow some of Chance's clothes. Jeans and a shirt. Socks, too."

Desi let out a laugh. "What on earth for?"

"Alex is here."

Desi's laughter died off with her blink. "Alex McCray?"

Reagan nodded vigorously. "He dropped in this afternoon and worked on my porch. I'm taking him to dinner, but he wanted to change. I can't stand the idea of *him* in Drew's clothes. Help me out, please?"

"Sure. I just did some laundry. It's on the kitchen island."

She disappeared inside her house, only to return in a handful of seconds, carrying a pair of stonewashed denim jeans and a heather green, collared tee. A pair of socks sat on the neatly folded bundle.

"Thanks, Des. I owe you big time." Reagan clutched the bundle to her chest. She turned to flee back to her house.

"Reagan?" Desi called after her.

She stopped in the open doorway. "Yeah?"

A warm smile lit up her best friend's face. "Don't be afraid to enjoy yourself. You do have needs. And we both know how long it's been."

Reagan snorted. "Right. He's Drew's best friend. So not going to happen. See you later, and thanks again!" Before Desi could offer more advice she didn't dare consider, she bolted back to her house.

As she slipped into her kitchen, Alex's voice rang out. "Reagan? Where'd you put those clothes?"

"Right here!" she called, hurrying up the stairs. "I'll set them outside the door."

"'Kay, thanks."

She put them on the floor and hurried into her bedroom to change as well. She freshened up after Alex left the bathroom.

Desi's words drifted through her mind as she stripped

out of her clothes. *Don't be afraid to enjoy yourself.* Was she afraid? What *if* Alex could separate sex from everything else? Could she?

The chances of something happening between them were about as likely as finding a genie in a bottle. But if opportunity arose, and she had to choose between always wondering what it would be like to have his body possess hers or taking what he offered, she could separate enough.

After all, it had been a long, *long* time since she'd wanted a man the way she wanted Alex. Wasn't it time to follow the advice of her counselor and live life? Sleeping with Alex didn't mean making commitments. It didn't *have* to be complicated.

Did it?

To hell with it all—she'd think herself into an even bigger mess. This was Alex, someone she knew well, and attraction aside, she enjoyed spending time with him. She wasn't going to screw up a night out with nerves and debating appropriate actions. She'd be herself. Like she'd been since the day she'd met him.

• • •

Alex made his way downstairs, tugging at the collar of his loaner shirt. It was a little tight across the shoulders and chest, and combined with his still-damp skin and the humidity in Reagan's un-air-conditioned house, it clung uncomfortably. The jeans were a good fit, at least.

He sank onto the sofa with a frown. The way Reagan had eaten him alive with her gaze still left his body overheated, despite the cool shower. How the hell was a man supposed to resist that sort of temptation? They'd been skirting around a simmering attraction for years, but there had always been an easy way to set it aside. Now, it was like setting a jar of chocolate mint cookies in front of him and telling him he could look and smell but not take a bite.

And he wanted a bite. He wanted a goddamn feast.

He reclined with a quiet groan and closed his eyes. The entire situation was just too weird for comfort. Drew's wife, his house, the memories of time spent here together waged war against the here and now and his damn honor. For Christ's sake, she was his late best friend's widow. He shouldn't have been attracted to her when Drew was alive, and he sure as hell shouldn't be attracted to her now.

Footsteps on the stairwell brought him out of his thoughts. He looked up, and his mouth went dry. She'd let her long strawberry hair down all the way, and it swung gently at her waist, shining in the light. Where she'd worn a casual T-shirt to work in the flower bed, she now sported a dressier sort of top. Short-sleeved, nothing that exposed a lot of skin — typical Reagan and yet alluring all the same. Paired with the lightweight white shirt was a denim skirt that hung low on her hips. And those legs, those heavenly legs that could make a man drop to his knees and beg, were accented by a pair of heeled sandals.

"Ready?" she asked as she reached the bottom of the stairs.

He stood, clearing his throat. Unable to find his voice, however, he merely nodded.

"Want to walk? It's nice out this evening, and the restaurant is just a few blocks away."

"Sure." Probably best — cooped up with her in a car,

where her light flowery perfume enveloped him, would only drive him over the edge. What the hell was it about this woman he couldn't resist?

Reagan beat him to the front door and pushed it open. Something clanged against the top of the frame, and she glanced up with a grimace. "Damn thing's going to fall down one of these days."

Joining her, he stepped out and gave the loose soffit board a quick once-over. Why hadn't she at least asked Chance to secure it temporarily? It was almost as if she thought it might simply go away. Pretending it didn't exist.

He pushed the nagging sensation aside, determined to enjoy the evening out, and made a mental note to brace the soffit up tomorrow. It would have to come off with the rest of the roof for anything more. Likely, she recognized that fact and put off doing anything with it until the whole situation could be addressed.

She ducked around him, her hair brushing against his elbow. He sucked in a sharp breath at the feathery caress, which only filled his head with her enticing scent. It reminded him of springtime flowers after a light rain. Innocence. Simple beauty.

Alex grimaced as he followed her down the steps. He'd never survive the evening if he didn't steer his thoughts elsewhere. There had to be something safe to discuss. Work. She was a teacher. Teachers were decidedly not sexy.

"So how did school go this year?" he asked.

She flashed a soft smile. "Pretty good. I had a really decent set of kids. They're at the perfect age, you know? No hormones interfering, and they've grown up enough to have real conversations."

Safe. Keep it up. He fell into stride at her side as they walked down the sidewalk toward the center of the town. "You like teaching, I take it."

"Oh, absolutely. But mostly I love the kids." She laughed quietly.

"I bet they love you, too." He blinked, unaware he'd uttered that sappy remark until it reached his ears. But it was true, he supposed. How could anyone not adore her? And he'd just bet that every eight-year-old boy harbored a crush.

Reagan gave a noncommittal shrug. Typical. She always downplayed herself.

"Seriously," he continued, "Remember that picnic or something we all went to a year or so ago when I came down from Chicago during leave?"

A frown touched her brow, and she nodded. "October Days."

"Yeah that. Those German sausages kicked ass. But the kids kept coming up to you, and you jumped in on a kickball game. All the kids wanted you on their team." The memory flashed in his mind. Her laughter. Her happiness. The way she'd had hugs for every child even when her hands had been full of cotton candy and soda. She'd been in her element, and he'd been mesmerized.

Reagan walked on, her expression one he couldn't interpret. Thoughtful, yet somehow tense. The light springtime breeze stirred her hair, and she grabbed it in one hand to keep it from blowing in her face. For an instant, he'd swear she'd gone someplace else.

But then her smile returned in full force, punching him in the gut when she turned it on him. "I have a soft spot for kids. Always have."

"But you and Drew—" He caught himself, not intending to take the conversation that direction.

Too late.

"No, we weren't trying for kids." Her voice lowered to a soft murmur. "It wasn't the right time."

"Yeah, I guess I can see that. Kinda hard to do the family thing with the husband overseas. Better to wait, since he wasn't a lifer."

"I'd rather not talk about Drew," she replied tightly.

Ouch. Yeah—exactly why he'd tried to stop that question. Talk about insensitive. She'd just buried her husband, for God's sake. He opened his mouth to apologize, but before he could utter a word, she rapidly turned the line of questioning on him.

"What about you? How come you've never settled down?"

Yipes. How to answer that when the explanation tied in with his attraction to her? There had been women, of course, but none of them elicited the same rush he felt when Reagan was around. "Guess I haven't met the right person." Lame, but better than the awkward truth.

"Not even come close, maybe?"

It was his turn to shrug. "There was someone," he allowed. "It wasn't meant to be." And that was as much of the truth as he was willing to reveal. He glanced around as they approached the retail heart of the small town. "So where is this place?"

She gestured at a brick building with decorative stone masonry around the windows and doors. "Right there."

"The Cock 'n' Bull Pub?" He wrinkled his nose. "What a name."

"It just opened around Christmas. You'll like it. Trust me." In a sudden unexpected move, she grabbed his wrist and dragged him through the door.

The urge to wrap his fingers around hers was too strong to resist, and he indulged in the feel of her soft skin against his palm. She didn't pull away. If anything, her grip tightened comfortably.

Too comfortably. Alex stole a glance at their joined hands as she spoke with the hostess. No interlaced fingers to imply intimacy, but the warmth of her fingers soaked into his soul. She felt good. This felt good. And if things were different, if there weren't a giant pink elephant wedged between them, he'd go after her with everything he was.

Chapter Four

To Alex's delight, the restaurant Reagan had chosen ended up being more of a bar. Music played at a tolerable level for easy conversation—some country, some pop, mainly anything with a danceable beat—and kept the dance floor busy. The atmosphere was lighthearted, exactly what he needed to rid his body of tension. And the beer selection surpassed what he'd expected out of the usual Colton bars, providing a wide variety of imports. Imports he'd sampled in alphabetical order by country.

At the moment, he was having trouble giving up the Weihenstephaner Hefeweissbier to leave Germany and move on down the alphabet. He sipped and eyed Reagan across the table.

She laughed over the top of her strawberry margarita. "Problem over there?"

Other than the fact he could only imagine how that strawberry would taste on her lips, no. He shook his head.

"Not sure I want to leave this little gem behind." He turned his bottle, indicating it.

"There's no way you can make it through the entire menu of a thousand brands tonight. Enjoy that one."

No, he certainly couldn't make it through the menu, but if he kept it up, he could pass out cold and be free of all the forbidden thoughts of her. Thoughts that had guttered and remained there from the time she took hold of his damn hand.

She glanced over her shoulder at the lively dance floor and looked back at him. Alarm bells began to buzz in his brain.

"Dance with me."

The alarms began to blare. *Danger, danger, contact imminent!* He spluttered his last sip of beer and frowned. "I don't dance."

"I call bullshit." She pushed her margarita aside and rose from the table. "You and Drew busted up the floor one weekend we went to Chicago."

Damn. She would have to remember that.

His excuse eradicated, he braced himself with a deep breath and accepted her offered hand. The burger he'd eaten hadn't offset the effect of the beers, and lightheadedness struck; he caught himself mid-stumble and managed to pull his balance back together before Reagan noticed. For half a second, he berated himself for letting his control slip, but then dismissed it all entirely. He felt good. Tipsy, but everything in his life right this second was just the way he wanted it. He'd deal with reality later. Like tomorrow morning.

She folded into his arms as if she'd been made to fit, and he had to swallow down a groan. Trim hips fell flush against his. Soft breasts compressed against his chest. Dainty fingers interwove with his. *Yeah. Like this.* Dipping his head and moving his feet in time to the slower rhythm, he indulged in the sweet scent that wafted off her skin.

"Mm." Reagan nestled closer. "Yeah, you know how to dance, liar."

He chuckled and fitted his free hand tighter against the small of her back. "Made it a point to learn before prom."

She tipped her chin up to look at him. Her sky blue eyes sparkled with amusement. "Hot date, huh?"

He arched an eyebrow. "It was prom. I didn't care about the *dance.*"

She laughed lightly, a musical sound that feathered across his skin and left chills in its wake. "Big plans after, then?"

At the memory of his overly cocky teenage self, he chuckled. "Oh, yeah. They crashed and burned. She left the dance with her first-choice date."

"Ouch." Reagan winced.

He shrugged. "Eh, she went to college and got hooked on cocaine. I'm better off without her." Running his chin over the top of her silky hair, he lowered his voice. Honesty slipped out before he could stop it. "If she'd stuck around, I wouldn't be dancing with you."

She wrapped her arms around his waist more securely and rested her cheek on his shoulder. "I guess I owe her a thank-you then. This is nice, Alex."

Yeah, it was better than nice. His heartbeat kicked up a notch as her body moved against his. She was so close. He'd waited what felt a lifetime for a stolen moment like this. To touch her. To stroke his fingers through her long, luscious hair. To feel her lips moving beneath his.

That wasn't going to happen. But the rest... He closed his eyes and gave in to the sweet indulgence, letting the music guide him. The atmosphere surrounding them shifted. Where light banter had entertained them all evening, something more serious, more *solid* laid fragile beginnings. She wasn't just Drew's widow and the woman who'd haunted him for too long to remember. She was *Reagan*. A vibrant young woman whom he admired and enjoyed. Whom he could talk to. Whom, if he didn't let his head get in the way, he could see himself spending a lifetime with.

The music shifted, a faster, upbeat tune replacing the lazy ballad. Reagan grabbed him by the hand and pulled him deeper into the crush of dancers. When he balked and she beckoned with a come-hither finger, flashing him an exaggerated sultry look, he threw his head back and laughed. It hit him then: when had he let loose and had fun like this? He couldn't remember. But damn, he was having a hell of a time. And sometimes, fully grieving meant completely letting go.

. . .

Reagan was still laughing when she and Alex left the pub just after eleven. It had been years, a decade at least, since she'd been able to go out, have fun, and not worry what sort of punishment she'd inadvertently earned. With Drew, the slightest glance from a stranger could have earned her his fists. Let alone what happened when he thought she gave his friends too much attention. Friends like Alex, whom she'd been careful to mind her behavior with even more. Though she hadn't always been able to avoid Drew's temper when it came to him anyway.

After his death, she'd tried going out. She kept Drew's secrets hidden so the town could have its hero. But the residents couldn't forget their Purple Heart awardee...or the widow who didn't grieve appropriately. Few faces offered welcome smiles. The Cock 'n' Bull Pub was one of a handful of exceptions, likely because the owner had lived here only four years and never knew Drew well. It became easier to stay in, to avoid the chilly shoulders. She'd have thrown in the towel and moved if it weren't for the kids, the job she loved, and an administration that believed in giving teachers the freedom to *teach*.

She pushed off the memories and turned to study Alex's profile as they walked down the street toward her house. Laugh lines around his mouth and eyes made him even more handsome in the moonlight. He carried himself with confidence, and the grip he maintained on her hand was comfortable. Not the possessive hold she'd become accustomed to.

She gave his hand a squeeze, bringing his mesmerizing gaze her way. "Thank you for tonight."

He returned the gentle clasp of her fingers and grinned. "Turns out Colton is more exciting than I'd realized, even after countless visits here."

"Kinda helps to move the action out of my backyard." Drew loved to barbecue and entertain around the grill and rarely took his guests out.

Alex raised an eyebrow playfully. "I don't know. The action in your backyard was pretty...eye-catching." He slowly raked his gaze down her body, then lifted it to her eyes once more.

Her heart stuttered violently. He was flirting. She'd wondered a few times throughout the night but hadn't been certain. Now, there was no doubt about it. But what did it mean? *He's been drinking. That's what it means. Don't read into it.*

Uncertain how to respond, she laughed nervously. "You weren't so bad yourself, you know."

His gaze locked with hers for a pulse-stopping moment, and then he looked ahead. Silence fell around them, not awkward, but heavy all the same. Was he thinking about how there had always been *something* between them they'd never dared explore? Or was he remembering the friend he'd lost?

Worse, had she spoiled the moment by trying to return his not-so-subtle flirtation?

She supposed it really didn't matter. They were still dancing around the attraction, and if she were smart, she wouldn't let it go any further. Soon enough, he'd realize she wasn't grieving as she should be, and like everyone else, he'd start asking questions. Questions she couldn't answer without destroying all Alex thought he understood about Drew. Let alone the risk that came in trusting him with her secrets. If he turned his back on her like Drew's family had, she'd be devastated.

They reached her front lawn, and Alex started up the walk to the porch. She followed, hating that the night had come to an end. It had been magical, and she'd never forget these few priceless moments she'd had in his company.

She reached to put her key in the door and drew in a deep, sorrowful breath. Why couldn't it be easier?

With a halfhearted pull, she opened the door and entered the moonlit room, then turned to lock it behind him.

Alex tugged her back around. The breeze floated through the open window, drawing a few strands of her hair across her cheek. He gently tucked them behind her ear. His gaze held hers, darkly intense and serious.

"God, you're pretty," he murmured.

A thrill shot all the way down to her toes, and her stomach fluttered. She knew better than to believe him, though—this was the alcohol talking. He'd never say something like this sober. Chuckling, she set a hand on his chest and gently pushed. "And you're drunk."

He captured her hand by the wrist and moved it to her side. A half step forward brought him a breath away from her body. His gaze dipped to her mouth, and he swallowed visibly before locking eyes with her once more. "No," he whispered. "I'm sober enough to know what I'm doing isn't right."

Before Reagan could respond, his lips dusted across hers. Her breath caught with a soft gasp. Her heart beating erratically, she froze, afraid if she exhaled too hard, the magic would shatter. It was happening. The one thing she'd wanted for far too long stood right in front of her. Could she embrace what he offered?

Yes. She could, and she would. One night, one magical night, to remember for a lifetime.

His teeth clasped her lower lip softly. A gentle nudge begged for entrance, and Reagan parted her lips and closed her eyes. His tongue traced the seam of her mouth, then dipped ever so slightly inside. She met the sweet invasion, coaxing him deeper, opening to him completely as she lifted her arms and wound them around his neck.

He held her in place with a firm hand on her hip and

maintained control over the slow, languorous kiss. But she could taste the thin edge of sharp desire with each stroke of his tongue. That barely restrained passion set her body on fire. Her hips shifted instinctually, brushing against the hard ridge of his cock.

A low, satisfied grunt rumbled in his throat. His grip tightened on her hip bone, and he eased off, his lips clinging to hers as if he didn't want to break apart. She captured his upper lip with her teeth, tugging him back. But instead of falling back into the kiss, he drew away. His ragged breath echoed between them as he lifted his free hand and pushed his fingers through her hair.

Regret flashed in his eyes. "And I'm tipsy enough to do it anyway. Damn. I'm sorry, Reagan. I shouldn't have—"

She tightened her hold around his neck at the same time she rose to her toes to brush her mouth over his. "It's... okay." She swallowed to gain a little control over her frenetic heartbeat. "Really okay. Do it again." Leaning in, she caught him in another brief kiss. "And don't stop, Alex. Don't stop."

Chapter Five

Something unlocked inside Alex at Reagan's whispered command. The gentle demand of her mouth made it impossible to remember why he was fighting, and God help him, he didn't care. He fastened his hands around her waist and navigated her backward to the sofa. Her hips rocked into his, arcing hot desire throughout his system. He tugged at her top to free it from the waistband of her skirt. He needed to touch. Needed to discover if her breasts were as full and soft as he'd imagined a hundred times or more.

He slid his fingers beneath the loose material and skated them over her flat abdomen. Her stomach tensed, and she sucked in a sharp breath. Slowly, he inched his way up her ribs, pushing the fabric higher, until his palms molded around the weighty fullness of her breasts. Soft. Definitely soft. And goddamn, they fit perfectly. A needy groan rumbled in his throat, and he tore his mouth from hers to trail kisses down the side of her neck.

When he ran his thumbs across the lace of her bra and stroked her pebbled nipples, she arched her back with a pleasured whimper.

That little sound destroyed him. Her perfume wrapped around his mind, the heat of her skin soaked into his hands, and his cock began to ache beneath the tight fly of his jeans.

"So perfect," he murmured against the side of her throat. "I've wanted to touch you like this since the day we met." He drew his thumbs over her nipples once more.

"Alex," she whispered, sliding one hand into his hair. Her nails scraped pleasantly against his scalp as she held him in place. Once more, her hips gyrated, this time more insistent.

He rocked into her, stroking himself through their layers of clothing. And again, as instinct overrode reason. It had been a while since he'd satisfied his needs, but damn, it hadn't been that long. He couldn't remember ever wanting a woman so fiercely.

Tugging her shirt a little higher, he bent his head lower, then reached behind her to unfasten her bra. Her breasts spilled into his hands, and he gave them a squeeze. At once, touch wasn't enough, and the moonlit darkness cloaked what he wanted to see. He lifted his head to glance around the room. "Where's the lamp?"

Reagan shook her head. "No lights."

He didn't have time for dismay to settle in. Her fingers nimbly freed the button on his fly, and one dainty hand slipped inside to wrap around his cock. White-hot fire shot through his veins as she worked him over. *Jesus.* He pulled in a hard breath, steeling himself against the rising need.

But he didn't stop her. Eyes closed, he measured his

breathing and let pleasure soak into all the empty places deep inside his being. Places he hadn't even realized existed until her talented fingers took command of his body. He'd be perfectly content to stand here until she milked him dry.

No, not content. Damn it. He wanted to know every bit of her by taste.

Reluctantly, he wedged a hand between their bodies and eased her away. Twining his fingers with hers, he gave in to a smile, and then dragged an openmouthed kiss across her shoulder. "Your fingers are dangerous."

She let out a light laugh and hooked an ankle behind his knee. Tumbling backward, she drew him down with her onto the couch. He braced an elbow on either side of her shoulders and gazed down at her impish grin. "Taking the reins, huh? You want to be on top?"

Her eyes went wide for a moment, and her laughter cut off. But in the next heartbeat, her smile returned. She shook her head. "I'm good right here. You feel amazing."

He smirked. "It would be better if we were both naked."

"Maybe you should fix that then."

"Mm." He dropped his mouth to her throat. "Maybe I should." Shifting his weight onto one elbow, he used a hand to grab the side of her shirt and work it up her body. He followed with the opposite, and then, with a little shimmy from her, dragged it over her head, along with her unfastened bra. His gaze fell to her exposed breasts. Her skin held a faint silvery hue from the glow of the moon, but only enough to highlight the contours of her curves. How he wished he could see them clearly. Wished he could watch her expression as he sucked one into his mouth and teased a hard nipple with his tongue.

But if scant moonlight was all he could have, he wouldn't ruin it with a complaint. Not that there was really anything to *complain* about. He had the woman of his dreams beneath him. He couldn't ask for more.

Navigating by feel, he scattered kisses down her body until he found the stiff bud of her nipple. When he drew his tongue over the top, Reagan turned her head aside with a muffled sound of pleasure. He might not be able to see her face clearly, but he could hear her, and he had the details memorized enough his mind could fill in all the rest. Her petal-pink lips would be parted. Her long sooty lashes would shutter her beautiful blue eyes.

Alex smoothed his hands down her rib cage to her skirt. Gathering the fabric in his fingers, he tugged one side up and shifted his weight. As he brushed his fingertips across the tops of her thighs, she parted her legs with another sexy little whimper. He lifted his head, trying once more to get a glimpse of her expression. "Tell me how you like it," he whispered as he slipped one fingertip beneath the scrap of cotton and stroked her wet center.

She arched her back and let out a quiet moan.

"Harder? Faster?" He raked his teeth across her nipple as he circled her clit.

"Softer," she murmured. Undulating against his caresses, she clutched at his shoulders. "Slower."

He moved in time with the gentle rise and fall of her hips. She was slick and hot, and the jagged little breaths she sucked in ratcheted up his breathing. He swept downward, over her opening, and dipped one finger inside. Reagan's legs parted further as she mewled again.

"Feel good?" he murmured as he dusted a light kiss

across the high swell of her breast. Simultaneously, he crooked his finger, hitting her in just the right place. She arched high off the couch, pressing hard against his hand.

With a side-to-side toss of her head, she released another soft, pleasured cry.

He dropped a knee to the floor and ran his tongue down the centerline of her body. Her sweet feminine scent filled his nose, and hunger punched him in the gut. Hard. He settled his mouth against her sex and swept his tongue through her wet folds.

"Alex," she moaned as she lifted into his mouth.

The sound of his name on her lips was more erotic than anything he'd ever experienced, and if it were possible, his cock hardened even more. He was painfully ready, but damn it, he was going to enjoy her awhile. He bit back the overwhelming need to give over to release and tongued her again.

Reagan writhed beneath him. When she rose off the cushions again, he cupped her ass in both hands and held her up to suckle her clit. Her hands latched into his hair, her nails digging almost painfully into his scalp. The sting only ramped up his desire. Her flavor filled his senses, and he swept his tongue lower to edge inside her opening. God, she was so sweet, so tantalizing. Thirty times better than the expensive imports he'd consumed all night.

As he slowly thrust inside her again, her body convulsed. She gave over to orgasm with a high-pitched keen.

Alex took his time in letting her go. If he did anything quicker, he'd tear off his clothes and slam into her. So he lapped at her folds, drinking her in, teasing her clit with gentle nips and tugs until her panting eased off, and she began to tilt her hips ever so slightly against his rhythm.

He licked her once more, long and slow, then pressed a firm kiss to her navel. "You're absolutely beautiful, you know that?"

She chuckled as she ran a hand tenderly over his shoulder. "You can't possibly say that when it's so dark in here."

"Oh, but I can. And you, *that*, was fucking beautiful." He edged back, away from the couch to rid them both of the rest of their clothing.

"I want all of you, Alex," she said, her fingers tightening around his bicep, as if she feared he might walk away.

He reached across his body, pulled her fingers free, and brought her hand to his mouth to kiss her knuckles. "It's a little easier to accomplish if you let me take my jeans off, baby doll."

"Oh. Yeah. That." A whisper of a laugh tumbled off her lips.

"Yeah, that." Still chuckling himself, he rose and shucked his clothes. But when he bent to pull her skirt down her legs, she stopped him with a flattened palm to his bare chest.

"Let me look a minute."

He stilled, one eyebrow arched and a smirk tugging at his mouth. "What happened to the whole dark thing?"

"Shh," she whispered as she lifted into an upright position. "I've wanted to do this for years. I can see enough."

Her lips skimmed across his chest like a feather's caress. Slowly, she scattered soft kisses across his shoulder to the tattoo on his bicep that he'd gotten after boot camp. Even more slowly, the tip of her tongue traced the black dagger and the words he had learned to live by—*Death Before*

Dishonor. Her warm breath scalded into his skin, making him close his eyes to the enormity of ecstasy that pumped through his veins. "Years?" he croaked out hoarsely.

"Years," she murmured before her tongue flicked across his nipple. Then she closed her mouth, and her teeth raked over his pectoral. One hand curved around his cock and slid down the length of his erection.

It was too much for his near-painful state of arousal. With a shuddering breath, he leaned into her, forcing her backward into the cushions. His body chased hers, his hips nestling between her parted legs. Her wet flesh cradled his cock, dealing a staggering punch that threatened to send him into blissful oblivion. But the heat of her body brought an even more shattering blow. His entire body tensed, and he froze in place. Damn! He couldn't be seconds away from the one thing he most wanted, only to have to walk away because he stupidly wasn't prepared.

He swallowed hard. "Reagan, I…didn't exactly foresee this happening. I don't have any—"

She trailed two fingers down the side of his face. "You know I'm clean, Alex, and I'm still on birth control."

The knot that had begun to form behind his ribs loosened. "I promise you I'm safe. I wouldn't be that selfish."

Her fingertips traced his mouth. "Kiss me," she whispered.

He obeyed and captured her in a hungry kiss. At the touch of her tongue, his self-restraint crumbled, and he nudged his hips forward, stroking himself against her slick sex. Pleasure rolled through his body. He desperately wanted this night to never end, but he'd slipped so far beyond control, he knew he didn't have hours in him. His body hurt in ways he couldn't define, ways he hadn't experienced before. And being inside Reagan was no longer a desire, but a physical need.

She seemed to sense his fraying willpower and lifted into him, aligning herself more completely with the tip of his cock. He reached between their bodies, fisted a hand around his shaft, and eased his swollen head inside. Reagan exhaled in a rattling hiss. In the next heartbeat, she moaned and wrapped her legs around his thighs, levering herself up and drawing him deep inside.

"Fuck," he muttered as he sank his forehead to her shoulder, temporarily rendered useless.

Her inner walls contracted around him, and she shimmied her hips, taking him as deep as he could go. The head of his cock pressed tight against her cervix. Her damp heat scorched clear through his skin. And Jesus, the way she gripped him—he groaned in ecstasy.

"My God, you feel good," she murmured as she canted her hips again.

He gathered his senses and pulled out slowly, inch by torturous inch. It was all he could do to remember to breathe, let alone chain his desire enough not to pound into her. She'd asked for soft and slow, but he was on the edge of that wildness. A heartbeat away from being nothing but a savage animal.

He bit into the side of his cheek and sank back into her, keeping his pace slow. When he was buried balls-deep, he stilled, sucked in a fortifying breath, and started the process all over again, just a little faster. Reagan kept pace with him, her hips rocking and falling in perfect counter-motion. Then she urged him faster. And faster. Until he forgot all about taking his time and slammed into her recklessly. His lungs squeezed together like they'd been locked in a vise.

Orgasm built steadily with every thrust, growing more out of control until it exploded through him. His cock jerked inside her as her body clenched around him. Blood roared through his ears as he bucked hard one last time. Dimly, he heard Reagan's scream of ecstasy, felt her shudder. Then, for a moment, he couldn't hear anything, couldn't see even the shadows in the room. Couldn't feel anything but the all-consuming throb of release.

Shaky, drained, and spent beyond his wildest imagination, he relaxed into her embrace and laid his cheek on her shoulder. For several long minutes, he listened to the sound of her ragged breathing. Her fingers played across the back of his shoulders, swept lazily up and down his spine. She turned her head to press a kiss to his damp forehead.

"No, Alex, *that* was beautiful."

Yes, it was. But he was too damned exhausted, too damned spent, to make the right words form. He secured his arm around her waist, closed his eyes, and cut off the nagging voice of reason that whispered in his ear, telling him he'd gone too far, crossed too many boundaries.

Chapter Six

A car engine drew Reagan from the blissful cocoon of sleep. She opened her eyes to the moon-kissed shadows of her living room. A firm weight held her legs to the sofa, and she glanced down her body to see Alex's thigh thrown over hers. His very bare thigh, resting against her exposed skin.

She was completely naked, and if she lay here until morning like she yearned to do, she'd never be able to keep her emotions at a distance. Worse, the truths she desperately didn't want him to discover couldn't be hidden in daylight. She'd never be able to save him from that horrible reality.

But the idea of pulling herself from beneath him and leaving the couch left her hollow inside. In his arms, the world had been…right. She'd been his. He'd been hers. And for a little while, the ghost that divided them was laid to rest. More than anything, she wanted to turn onto her side, nestle against his big strong body, and burrow her nose into the side of his neck while she breathed in the scent of him.

Hell, she was fooling herself—her emotions were already tangled up in Alex McCray. She never wanted to let go of this moment, longed to hold on forever. He made her happier than she'd been in years—tonight had been so fun, so relaxing, so normal.

Yet, she couldn't hold on forever. The one bit of happiness she'd found was forbidden to her.

Sorrow rose, bringing tears to her eyes. She swallowed hard to keep them at bay. Taking care not to disturb him, she eased off the couch. With even greater care, she kept her back facing away from him as she gathered her clothes, just in case he woke, then backed four steps to the darker stairwell. When she reached the thicker cover of shadows, she turned and took the stairs two at a time, past the master bedroom, to her smaller room at the end of the hall.

Once locked inside, she gave in to emotion. It was so unfair. Even now, from the grave, Drew managed to control her. He'd been an abuser, and the whole damn town revered him as a hero. She'd kept his secrets. She'd even gone so far as to ask Drew's sister Shelley whether she thought counseling might help him. Shelley had spilled the beans, and somehow, Drew managed to convince his entire family Reagan had mental issues and had made it all up. The only real family she'd had turned against her.

She sank down the door to sit on the floor and buried her face in her hands. Mental issues—she'd paid for betraying Drew's secret. Now, after the bruises, the blood, the attacks on her character had all stopped, she was still paying for it. Because no doubt about it, once Alex woke, he wouldn't be happy about having sex on her couch. His honor would rise up screaming and punish them both.

And if she sat him down to tell him the truth... She couldn't. Not that she was really considering confiding in him and opening herself to a gut-wrenching rejection. But if she did, and if he believed...

No. Regardless of her pathetic marriage, he and Drew had been best friends. Drew had died protecting Alex. Hell, he wore the creed they'd sworn to uphold permanently affixed to his arm. Honor came before everything.

"Goddamn you, Drew," she choked through her tears. She drew a shuddering breath and forced herself to her feet. Crying solved nothing. Especially when there was nothing to solve. She had no future with Alex without the truth. She couldn't hide the scars in darkness forever, couldn't dodge the innocent questions, and she refused to pretend at life anymore. And frankly, she wasn't ready to chance letting someone in that close again only to suffer the heartbreak of betrayal.

She curled onto her bed, feeling the same old hopelessness clinging to her shoulders. She hadn't experienced that oppressive weight since Drew's death, and she'd thought she would never know it again.

She'd been wrong.

Tears fell harder, and she turned her face into the pillow to quiet her sobs. She hated that he still had the ability to make her cry, to make her weak. But tonight she'd tasted true happiness, known what it felt like to be truly wanted. And damn it, she was sick to death of pretending.

• • •

Alex reached over the edge of the couch for his boxers.

Head still fogged from a mind-numbing orgasm and one too many beers, he stared at the stairwell, listening to Reagan's muffled crying.

He was an asshole. A bastard. What kind of man honored his best friend's memory by fucking his wife?

Nor had he stopped to consider that Reagan was a grieving widow. He'd selfishly taken what she'd offered. Now, when he ought to be comforting her, he didn't dare go to her. He didn't belong at her side, not when he'd made everything awkward and uncomfortable.

He ran a hand over his hair and blew out a hard breath. If he were sober, he'd get in his car and leave. She might be pissed, but it would be better than what promised to come with the morning when they had to look at each other. Confront the reality all over again—not that she evidently faced reality as it was. Still, she'd heal a hell of a lot faster without him around to complicate everything.

Christ, he shouldn't have listened when she'd said it was okay. It wasn't okay. *She* wasn't okay. Clearly. Every time Drew came up, she dodged the subject. She bottled her grief up and hid it away.

Just like he did.

But no matter how he wanted to bolt out that door, he couldn't turn his back on her. She needed help. Stubbornness, avoidance, whatever it was, her damned house was virtually falling apart. She had even allowed a second-rate contractor to take advantage of her. He'd be ten times the asshole if he let that happen again.

He twisted onto his side and stared at the armchair where Drew had always sat. He could almost see him there now, a beer in hand as he cheered on the Rams. The memory burst forth in vivid color. Drew's deep voice belting over the television announcer. Reagan sitting in the chair beside him when she wasn't in the kitchen making appetizers and snacks. Drew and him passionately criticizing the quarterback.

It had been almost a family for Alex. Too many years divided his sister and him; she'd left for college when he was only nine. His brother had never shared his love of sports, following more in the way of his parents' and sister's love of the arts.

Until Alex met Drew in boot camp, he'd never really known the bonds of brotherhood. The days he'd spent in this dinky little town during leave, throwing the football around in Drew's backyard with Chance, barbecuing on the grill, kicking it back. Damn, he missed his best friend. And what he'd done tonight with Reagan changed all those memories.

It made the occasional lingering glance they'd shared seem traitorous. Made the way she innocently paid him no attention seem deliberate. Like they'd been hiding something.

Worse…down deep where the ache started, Alex wanted to do it all over again.

Which made him even more selfish. For Christ's sake, he'd sunk so far from honor it was shameful. She deserved a better man. He punched a fist into the cushion and swore beneath his breath. Tomorrow, he was cutting the last of that tree off her roof. He'd secure the dangerous parts of her front porch and then help her line up reputable contractors to fix the rest of the things she needed. He didn't dare wait another day—he couldn't trust himself to stay.

Chapter Seven

"Shit!"

Reagan's oath jerked Alex out of sleep. He blinked, groggily, and then scrubbed his eyes, momentarily confused about his surroundings. The scent of something burning cleared the fog. He lifted onto one elbow, peering through the entry to the kitchen with a frown.

A pan clattered. Followed by more of Reagan's mumbling, but he couldn't make out what she said. Running water rushed in the sink just as the smoke detector began to beep. His head pounded with each shrill note.

Muttering to himself, he pushed off the couch to investigate the commotion. He glanced at his shirt lying in a rumpled heap on the floor, then thought better of putting the uncomfortably tight thing on. He supposed it didn't really matter—much as he'd like to erase his behavior last night, he couldn't, and Reagan had seen everything he had to offer anyway.

Alex found her in the kitchen, standing at the counter, glaring at a pile of something black and charred on a plate. Her hair still mussed from sleep, she wore merely a faded old T-shirt and a pair of sleeping shorts. Plain and natural, she looked sexy as hell. Damn it. He didn't need to start his morning with a shot of desire, much less a pounding headache.

"Problems?" he grumbled over the ear-splitting beeps, one hand held to his temple.

She jumped, but surprised him with a grin. "I forgot about the bacon. Sorry, didn't mean to wake you."

Uncertain what to make of her bright and cheery disposition, he stalked to the headache-inducing noisemaker and snatched the battery out. Blessed silence filled the room. He took a deep breath, calming his sensitized nerves.

When he turned around, Reagan had a glass of what looked to be tomato juice in her extended hand.

"Here, have a V8."

He wrinkled his nose.

She pushed it a little closer. "It'll help with the hangover."

"I don't have a—" Frowning, he accepted the glass. There was no reason to deny his shame. Hell, it was almost a serviceable excuse for the way he'd all but attacked her the minute they walked through the front door last night. It was certainly well-deserved punishment.

Bracing himself for the terrible taste, he tipped it to his mouth, downed half the glass, and set it on the counter. The reflexive grimace was impossible to control. God, he hated tomato anything.

Why was she so chipper? He was pretty sure she'd cried herself to sleep before he finally dropped off again last night.

The last thing he'd expected to wake up to was Reagan acting like everything was normal. Like they hadn't had mind-blowing sex on her couch.

Drew's couch.

Then again, he shouldn't be surprised. Since he'd arrived, she'd acted like nothing had happened. *Avoidance. Plain as day.*

He shoved the internal voice aside and gritted his teeth. "Bacon for what?"

Reagan waved a dismissive hand as she turned back to the charred food. "I was going to make a casserole for tonight."

The thought of food made his stomach twist. Best not to shake it up by continuing that line of conversation. He carefully eased himself into a chair at the oak-finished bar that separated the dining table from the expansive kitchen. In the distance, thunder rumbled. Alex glanced out the back patio doors at the gray sky. Damn, a storm would only set him back and prevent him from leaving.

Silence gnawed at him as she tinkered around in the kitchen, grabbing things from the fridge, putting them back, dragging bowls from the cabinets, and clanking around at the sink. It seemed hours stretched out of a few minutes. He knew he ought to say something, but what, exactly, eluded him.

Finally, he decided to give it a try. Anything was better than the lame-ass, obvious quiet. "About last night, Reagan."

She turned around, a large plastic spoon in one hand, and gave him an adamant shake of her head. "Don't you dare apologize. That's worse."

So she *was* upset—he didn't need any more confirmation. He heaved a sigh and drummed his fingers on the countertop as she went back to whatever it was she was working on.

Screw this—she wasn't escaping this conversation. And he wouldn't chicken out. Things needed to be said. "He was my best friend, Reagan. I can't just forget all the time we've been together, the three of us. Look me in the eyes and tell me what we did last night doesn't bother you to some degree."

She spun again, a frown marring her pretty face. She began to answer, then evidently thought better of it, closed her mouth, and shrugged.

Damn it.

Another clap of thunder made the house shake. Rain crashed into the sliding glass door. Buckets of rain. Reagan's frown deepened. "I have more pressing things to worry about than any sort of guilt, Alex."

With that sharp retort, she bent to the cabinet beneath the sink, pulled out a large soup pot, and dashed out of the room. He twisted in his seat, watching as she set the pot on the floor in her front room. No sooner had she set it down than a telltale *plink* rang out.

Fuck. Her damaged roof. She was right—more important things needed consideration. Namely the chaotic state of her affairs. But her sharp tone warned him now wasn't the time to broach that subject.

He pushed off his high-top chair and went to retrieve his clothes from the front room. "I'm going to run to the hardware store. Is there anything you need while I'm out?"

She glanced at him, surprise widening her eyes. She cleared her expression quickly, though, and nodded. "I could use a gallon of milk." She took a breath, then hurried to add, "If it's not any trouble."

He gave her a quizzical look. "I offered, didn't I?"

"Uh, yeah, but…"

"But what?" Damn, she was walking on eggshells around him. They *needed* to talk about what had happened…and everything else.

More quietly, she added, "My problems aren't yours, Alex."

Annoyance flared to life. As she tried to skirt around him, he grabbed her by the arm. "Damn it, Reagan, Drew saved my *life*. You think I'm just going to let the most important person in *his* life suffer? I owe it to him to make sure you're okay. You're not. Yet you're pretending like you are."

She jerked free of his hold. Her glare was immediate and scathing. "So that's what this is—pity? Was last night a pity fuck, too? You gave in because I asked?"

"Jesus! No!" He ran a hand down his unshaven face. "I wanted you. I want you still, and I feel like I'm cheating on Drew!" There, it was out. The god-awful truth of it. "He died *for me*, and the minute he's gone, here I am chasing after his girl. A girl I've always wanted but had to hide that attraction from my best friend. And you're acting like Drew was never part of your life. Add it all together, and yeah, I feel pretty shitty about everything. Can't you see that? Can't you understand?"

She merely looked at him, her expression a torrent of conflicting emotions.

The dam had burst, and Alex couldn't hold everything in. "He's not even here, where he should be. Where's his flag on the wall? Where's his woodworking stuff?"

"I sold it," she murmured. "Well, the woodshop. The flag's in the attic. I thought—"

"You thought what?" he snapped. His fucking flag was in the *attic*. Forgotten like the rest of him throughout the house. Put away where she wouldn't have to confront it.

"I thought you might want it," she answered, her voice barely audible over another roll of thunder. "You were there, too."

That soft phrase and the pain etched into her face was like a kick to the gut. His anger faded, and he blew out a hard, frustrated breath.

"I'm not dense, Alex," she continued. "I won't ever forget Drew, and I know his death tears you apart. But this is what I have left—a house that's broken and a life to rebuild, however possible." She looked like she wanted to say more, but instead, she turned and quietly made her way back to the kitchen.

"But you're not rebuilding," he responded flatly.

She stopped mid-stride, her shoulders as rigid as stone. He waited for her to whirl around, to give him a good what-for. But she didn't. Instead, she continued walking, her stride full of purpose, like he'd never said anything at all.

Damn, damn, *damn*. This was ridiculous. He refused to allow her to avoid *him*. He followed, tugging his shirt on as he walked. "Look—"

She kept her back to him. "There's a box of things in the attic you might look through while you're here. It's too hard for me to look at them, especially the Purple Heart. I don't have any children to pass the things on to, and you were with him for everything. The awards probably have more meaning for you."

Goddamn. She didn't want any of it? It killed him that her way of moving forward meant erasing Drew. He checked his immediate spike of anger. Grief impacted others in different ways—a lesson he'd learned more than once in his years in the service. He had no right to condemn. Her tears last night were proof enough she wasn't coldhearted or completely immune to Drew's death.

A long moment of silence spanned between them. A moment Alex realized he could never fill the right way. He could never replace Drew. She'd confessed the reminders were too hard to confront. Which, though she hadn't come right out and said it, implied he was a reminder, too. He would always be a reminder. Always be the one who'd survived, when she'd lost everything.

His shoulders slumped. "I'm going to the hardware store."

She continued to chop at something on her cutting board.

She'd lost her hero. And Lord knew, even if he could move beyond the guilt, he was a sorry substitute for a Purple Heart recipient. Screw his promise—he couldn't cope with her method of grieving. It pained him too much. He'd finish the roof, find a handyman, and then take off.

He returned to the front room to finish dressing, then left without another word. The rain made him feel a little better—today just wasn't a sunshine kind of day—and he took his time driving to the hardware store that was more of a little-bit-of-everything general store.

The weather had let up by the time he arrived. He entered and spotted an aging clerk behind the counter. Drew had called him Don.

Hoping the man wouldn't recognize him, he nodded cordially and wound his way down the aisles to the small section of overpriced clothing. He couldn't take another minute in this too-tight shirt.

After stuffing a comfortable T-shirt under his arm, he found a pair of serviceable jeans in his size and took them to the counter to ask about shingles and roofing supplies.

The old man strolled to the counter to meet him. His blue eyes were warm and friendly. "Need anything else?"

Alex tamped down a groan and said a silent prayer that the man wasn't into casual conversation. "Had a tree fall on a shake roof. Sheared off the front corner of shingles, cracked the plywood beneath. I've got a contractor coming out, but"—he gestured at the light rain outside—"I need something in the interim."

The man cocked a head of thinning gray hair, and those blue eyes studied him thoughtfully. "Must be working on the Sanders house. Weren't you in here with Drew a while back?"

The groan he'd been holding down rumbled softly. "Yeah. We served together."

Alex knew the moment Don put two and two together and connected with Drew's death. His expression smoothed with unmistakable sympathy.

"Damn shame what happened to you boys over there. I served my time in 'Nam, and I've been in your shoes. It never quite goes away." He thrust out a bony hand in an offered shake. "Welcome home, son."

Uncomfortable, Alex shook. "Thanks," he mumbled.

"Always an honor to shake a fellow soldier's hand." He motioned for Alex to follow toward the back corner of the store. As they walked, Don rambled. "People consider Sanders quite the hero, given the Purple Heart and all. Way

I heard it, all of you took heavy fire, and he wasn't the only one who saved some lives."

"Something like that," Alex mumbled. A flash memory surfaced—two young Afghan boys trapped in the corner of the street, caught in the cross fire, screaming for their mothers. He'd taken one look at Drew, and they'd both known Alex couldn't, *wouldn't,* leave those kids to die. He'd darted out from cover. Drew followed on his heels…

Alex shook off the flashback before it could consume him.

The old man studied him thoughtfully. "His wife seems to be coping with his death pretty well."

Too well. As the thought registered, Alex got a good look at the old man's expression. Speculation registered there. The hint that Alex wasn't the only one who'd observed something off with Reagan. Loyalty to her, and to the man who'd saved his life, kept him from indulging in gossip. "She's coping."

He nodded as he reached for a product booklet. "Her house is a wreck after that storm. Thought I might donate some materials. But my wife…" He shrugged as he flipped the booklet open. "Well, she's old-fashioned. Didn't think too kindly of the poor girl selling off her late husband's things the way she did. Can't rock the boat too much at home, you know."

Abruptly changing the subject, the vet looked over his shoulder with a conspiratorial wink. "You should stop by the VFW while you're in town. The boys and I will give you a real hero's welcome, if you know what I mean."

Yeah, that wasn't going to happen in this lifetime. He wasn't a hero. Not by any stretch. He'd been content with the likely price of his actions, accepting that saving those two kids would leave him dead. But Drew had followed...

The air felt thin, and Alex gripped the corner of a shelving unit to steady himself.

"You okay, son?"

Alex forced out a chuckle. "Skipped breakfast."

He could tell the old man didn't believe him, but there was something in the quiet way he assessed Alex. Something Alex only witnessed from other soldiers who'd seen the worst man had to offer and lived to watch another day, bearing healed scars that never quite stopped aching.

Don gave Alex a short nod and pointed at an overhead display of asphalt shingles in a wide array of colors. "I'd put these in if you're waiting on a contractor. I've seen the house. Experience says there's more structural damage than what's visible, and the whole roof will have to go. No sense spending the money on the expensive shake, if it's got to come off."

Alex nodded. "Easy to put up? I've never worked on a roof before."

"Easy as pie. Just fit them under the shake, as high as you can get them. Start at the bottom, overlap up. You got your work cut out for you."

As far as Alex was concerned, the more work the better. It might take him all day, but up on the roof, he'd be far enough away he couldn't make the mistake of touching Reagan again. "Thanks."

The old man scribbled something on a scrap of paper. "Give this to Ricky up front. He'll radio it to the shed—you'll have to drive around the side for loading."

Alex clasped the paper.

The old man held on. "Son, no one can pretend nothing happened. Talk it out. It's the only way to heal." He released his hold on the paper and shuffled away.

As Alex stared after him, a question nagged in the back of his mind. Was he talking about him? Or was he referring to Reagan?

Chapter Eight

Reagan bent over the pile of laundry on the coffee table and fished around until she found the couch cover. After last night's escapade, it had really needed a good wash. But she wasn't thinking about last night. Nope. Not happening. She refused to replay the delicious feel of Alex's hands on her body one more time. If she didn't think about how alive he'd made her feel, she couldn't be disappointed over the dead end they'd eventually come to. The one they may have already reached. Particularly given the way he'd seemingly taken charge of her disaster of a front porch and his attempt at telling her how to grieve. She'd just escaped one man who'd refused to relinquish control. If Alex thought he could come in here and take over, she wouldn't put up with it.

She shook out the cover and tugged it over the arm just as his pickup rolled into the drive. Her traitorous heart skipped a beat, and she froze in place, watching through the window as he headed for the front door.

When the doorknob rattled, she resumed her work. Playing it cool. As she had this morning. Ignoring the elephant in the room.

"Hey, I found some shingles," he said as he shut the door behind him.

Evidently, he was ignoring it, too. She nodded, biting back the immediate retort that he hadn't asked for her input. "What kind?"

He blinked. "Asphalt for the moment. It's just a temporary patch."

"Oh." So maybe he wasn't taking control, just doing what he was able, when she clearly couldn't. "Thank you."

He held up a gallon of milk. "You want this in the fridge?"

The milk. At that insignificant little detail, her heart melted into a puddle at his feet. No, he certainly wasn't Drew. She could count on one hand the number of times Drew had picked up something she needed, much less something she wanted. She gave Alex a smile. "Please."

Bending over the couch again, she looked up through the tops of her lashes, trying not to make it evident that she couldn't take her eyes off him. The man had a damn fine backside. Not just his tight ass but the whole picture — broad shoulders, narrow waist, perfect butt, and muscular legs. He was a walking embodiment of strength and confidence.

When he disappeared into the kitchen, she stuffed the opposite corner of the couch cushion into the elastic that held the fabric in place. The side she'd already affixed popped free. It was going to be one of those days. She sighed and went back to the opposite end.

"You want some help with that?"

Help? She almost didn't know what to do with the offer.

It took a minute, but she managed to nod. "Th-thanks," she stammered.

He arched an eyebrow but said nothing as he grabbed the opposite corner. Quietly, they worked together, cramming the poufy cushions into the tight covering. When she'd smoothed out the last of the wrinkles, Alex gestured at the remaining pile of sheets and blankets. "Can I help with that?"

Entirely unaccustomed to his charming offers of assistance, she floundered for a moment, and merely blinked. "Um."

"Are you okay?" Concern reflected in his fathomless green eyes.

"I'm fine." Just a little off-kilter. Like she'd stepped into some alternate reality. "I can get it."

"I'm sure you can. But I'm standing right here, and it's still sprinkling. Might as well lend a hand."

"In that case…" She tossed him a pillowcase. "Can you fold?"

He caught it with a swipe of his arm. "Did I spend six years in the marines?"

Reagan grinned. "I bet your corners put mine to shame."

"Guaranteed." He tossed her a wink, a welcome glimpse of the lighthearted man she'd always known.

"I thought I'd wash some blankets, in case you want to crash again."

Nodding, he continued to fold, but remained conspicuously silent. Her gut twisted. Instinctually, she knew he wasn't planning to stay. She shouldn't care — it was better if he left. Better for both of them.

Yet, she couldn't ignore the disappointment that shot through her nor the little voice that continually asked,

"What if?" Surely, he wouldn't react like Drew's sister and believe she'd made the abuse up, especially now that she had the scars to prove it. When Drew wasn't in the middle of them, they were remarkable together.

He was worth the chance. She couldn't just let him walk away. If she did, she'd regret it the rest of her life. If she could just puncture his barriers, she might be able to make him see they might really amount to something. But...how? His walls were impenetrable. His honor nothing less than a ten-inch-thick steel barricade.

"I had a chat with Don at the hardware store," Alex said after a few minutes.

"Oh?" Uh-oh. That couldn't be good. Don's wife was one of those people who asked questions. Too many. And Reagan's attempts at hiding Drew's secrets only resulted in the nosy woman's condemnation. Damned if she did, damned if she didn't.

Alex smoothed the crisp folds on the pillowcase and set it on the arm of the couch. He grabbed a fluffy red blanket and passed her two corners. "He said Drew's a hero around here."

Reagan's hands faltered, and she dropped one corner. *Hero.* Damn it. The subject pained her more than any gaping wound. "Yeah," she murmured. "Colton has a Purple Heart hero." *Watch the sarcasm.*

"You didn't tell me."

"Tell you what?" She caught the sharp edge to her voice and drew in a steady breath.

"That they thought so highly of him."

With a wary glance his way, she replied, "I didn't think it was necessary. He died for his country. This is Colton. I figured you'd already know. Have you thought about what you might want to do for dinner tonight?"

Alex stilled, mid-fold. His gaze narrowed.

Crap.

"How come every time he comes up, you dodge the subject?"

The words came out before she could stop them. "Because he's in the middle of us."

• • •

Alex blinked. Hard. He stared at Reagan, trying to process her statement. She was Drew's *widow.* How in the world could she be so…cold? It was like she didn't even miss him. *Like he never existed.*

As annoyance flickered, he gritted his teeth. "There isn't an us, Reagan."

"Maybe there would be." Her voice flat and even, she continued to sift through the laundry, as if she were talking about something as mundane as the weather.

"No, there can't be." Shaking his head, he let out a hiss. Then, more calmly, he said, "I'm not going to be the man everyone sees as poaching in Drew Sanders's backyard. Don't you get it?"

"Get what, exactly? That you're too wrapped up in guilt to enjoy something that's right here? Or that you're determined to punish us both?"

He balled the washcloth and pitched it on the ground. "Damn it, no! It's about honor. And it's like we're cheating on him."

She stuffed her hands on her hips. "Are we supposed to

die along with him? Is that how honor works?"

He looked away, unable to face her. The idea of accepting that logic filled him with shame. It was true, and yet, some part of him he didn't understand couldn't admit it.

"The last time I checked, neither you nor I was in the grave. We didn't *cheat* on Drew. We aren't cheating on him now."

"We're cheating on his memory," he murmured.

"Bullshit. Do you expect me to never be in a relationship again? To *honor* his memory by living like a nun?"

He gritted his teeth and lifted his gaze, his eyes narrowing. "Don't twist this."

"Twist it?" she scoffed. "You're too afraid to live. Too afraid you might find some happiness. Which was why he threw himself on that grenade, by the way, because he wanted *you* to go on living." She glared at him, challenge glinting in her eyes. Daring him to deny it.

"And he damn sure didn't expect me to do that with you!"

"You don't know that. You don't know half of what you think you do about him. He—" She snapped her mouth shut, and her eyes widened, and then she shook her head and snatched another sheet out of the pile. More calmly, she continued, "You're making assumptions."

Oh, no. No way was she getting out of that so easily. "What the hell do you mean, I only know half of what I think I do?"

"Nothing."

"It's something, Reagan."

"It's *nothing*," she gritted out tightly.

"You know what? Forget it. You might be able to

pretend he didn't exist, but he was like my brother." His anger got the better of him, and words came out in a furious bellow. "I got shot at beside him. I watched men die—our friends—beside him. I watched him put everything on the line to protect them time and again. Damn it, I held him as he bled out. Don't you *dare* tell me I didn't know him! He was a fucking hero, and his *wife* can't even give him the loyalty and respect he deserves."

Alex spun on his heel and stormed to the door. That sealed it; he was out of here. He'd fulfill his promise to Drew, and he was done. Done with the guilt. Done with the arguing, and done with the fucking temptation of Reagan.

Chapter Nine

Reagan sat on the couch, staring at the broken front window, half listening to the rhythmic hammering overhead. It was more of a monotonous cadence that kept her thoughts from spinning out of control, as opposed to a conscious sound. Alex's parting words, though he'd spewed them a couple hours ago, still cut deeply.

His wife can't even give him the loyalty and respect he deserves.

Loyalty...she knew the meaning. And if Alex had half an idea of the kind of loyalty she'd shown Drew by keeping his darker side quiet, he'd come apart at the seams. More than anything, she wanted to tell him the truth about her marriage. But doing so would be selfish. It would only be a means to ending her pain, a way of correcting his false perception of *her*. She'd rather be the heartless bitch he thought she was than hurt him.

At the same time, the guilt he wore so obviously nagged

her to come clean. It was even less fair to let him berate himself needlessly when she could put an end to it. Maybe then, what divided them would draw them together.

But what if he didn't believe her? What if, like Drew's sister, Alex thought she'd concocted the whole story? At one time, Shelley and she had been like sisters. Close enough that Reagan had felt comfortable taking her into confidence in hopes there was something that might help Drew. Like a rabid dog, she'd turned on Reagan viciously.

Or would Alex react like the townspeople, pulling back when they couldn't make sense of her reactions. Would he, too, distance himself and treat her like some sort of...freak? She'd learned how to cope with the less-informed, and she wasn't willing to run away from Colton as if she had something to be ashamed of. But if Alex reacted the same way, Reagan didn't trust that she wouldn't end up right back in her counselor's chair. She'd come so far from that place of hopelessness and despair she couldn't risk falling back into the patterns.

Then there was the matter of Drew's hero status. Alex was right—he'd died for others. She'd been told the entire story: the unit drew heavy fire on a surprise attack. Alex and Drew became separated from the others. Stuck in a hut while the rest of their team was in the hot seat on the rooftop overhead. When a grenade sailed through an open doorway, Drew jumped on it to spare the entire unit. Not many soldiers would have done that, she had to admit. She even had to admit it had bothered her for a while that *strangers* could provoke such kindnesses from him, when she, his *wife*, couldn't.

But she'd come to accept that the soldier had been

different from the man. And while the soldier might deserve a hero's memory, the man had been a piece of shit.

Unconsciously, she ran a hand over the back of her shoulder, fingering the unmistakable proof. She wasn't even aware she was doing so until a tingle shot down her arm. Annoyed by the habit, Reagan dropped her hand to her lap and wedged it under her thigh. One of these days, the subconscious part of her brain would accept the scars weren't going away, and disbelief would fade.

How the hell had she gotten into this situation with Alex? And how the hell did she make it right?

You have to tell him.

But wasn't it kinder to leave him to his illusions? Let him go on believing the man he regarded so highly was honorable and noble?

No, he needed to know.

The hammering overhead stopped, an irregular break in the noise. She glanced at the ceiling, picturing Alex on the roof, hammer in one hand, sweat glistening on his bare shoulders. If she didn't find a solution quick, the only thing she'd end up accomplishing was his hating her.

She pushed off the couch, driven to restlessness by the constant thrum of questions in her head and the oppressive humidity in her house. Morning rain had given way to scorching afternoon heat. A shower would work wonders on her mind.

And maybe, just maybe, if she cooled off, she'd find the right words to explain.

· · ·

Alex thumped the hammer against the roof and rocked onto his heels, stretching his back. The physical labor had gone far in diffusing his anger. He shouldn't have yelled at Reagan. For all he knew, avoidance was her coping mechanism. Instead, he'd pressed her. Worse, he'd flat-out insulted her.

But what the hell had she meant that he didn't know Drew?

He scowled. Something wasn't right. Reagan and Drew had been the happiest couple he'd ever seen. They had the perfect marriage, so long as he didn't think too hard about the way she'd looked at him in stolen, fleeting moments. Sure, Drew had the normal complaints about Reagan spending too much money, but he'd never voiced anything more serious, never truly bitched, never expressed any sort of unhappiness.

So why was she bottled up so tight? What was she hiding?

And where the hell was her life insurance money? With her salary and the death benefits the marines provided, she should have been able to find a reputable roofer. And the house—how had it come to this? Surely, she and Drew had credit she could have used for the air-conditioning.

Come to think of it, where was Drew's family? Reagan had cut all ties with hers before she married—evidently her parents had been a half step up from junkies on the street— but she'd been close to the Sanders clan. Sure, they were farther north, closer to the lake, but not so far they couldn't help.

Yeah, something was definitely not right. Maybe her spending habits were more of a problem than Drew let on. Maybe that's why she'd sold his tools. Maybe that's why his family and the town distanced themselves.

Time for some answers.

He set the hammer aside, dumped a handful of nails into a plastic pail, and then crawled down the ladder. As soon as his foot touched the grass, the one remark she'd made that he couldn't shut out drifted through his mind again. *Are we supposed to die along with him?*

He gripped the ladder tight, squeezing his eyes shut as something foreign and uncomfortable kinked behind his ribs. She was absolutely right—they weren't dead. Life couldn't come to a stop because Drew had passed. They—*he*—couldn't stop functioning, and it would be natural for Reagan and him to come together as they had. Were they really cheating on his memory?

He couldn't answer.

Besides, once she learned he was responsible for Drew's death, all this would come to a shattering end. She'd recognize she'd already had the better man and wash her hands of him. He'd let her too far under his skin already to think her rejection wouldn't tear him to pieces.

Shaking off the discomfort, he pushed aside the intense attraction between them and focused on the tangible issues—answers. If some red tape issue had locked up the insurance and put Reagan in this position, Alex could make some phone calls and likely have it cleared up in a short while. If she'd run through the money…well, he'd figure out a solution.

He strode to the door, more calm and relaxed than he'd felt since his arrival. This he could navigate. This wasn't threatening. This didn't make him feel like he'd just climbed on a roller coaster and pitched down a towering hill at mach speed.

Alex wiped the sweat off his brow on his sleeve and opened the rickety front door. He stopped, dead in his tracks, halfway inside.

Reagan sat in the armchair facing the door, dressed in only a plain white bra and a pair of loose cotton shorts. Her wet hair hung over her shoulder in clumps, and she flipped through a magazine. She'd moved a fan into the room, positioning it so it circulated on her. From the way she focused on the ruffling pages in her hand, he got the distinct impression she wasn't expecting him to come inside any time soon.

"Ah…" He stumbled for words. Little rivulets from her hair trickled down her collarbone, over the high swell of her breasts, and into her bra. The wet material clung to her skin, molding around a tight nipple. The memory of that little bud rolling beneath his tongue slammed into him. Her sexy little whimpers ricocheted through his head.

She looked up without the faintest trace of surprise, blowing his suspicion he'd caught her off guard.

"We should talk." She tossed the magazine onto the coffee table. "There are…things…you should know." Shifting position in her chair, she stared down at her hands, rubbed the back of her knuckles, and paused a long moment. Then, shaking her head as if arguing with herself, she looked up, her expression determined. "I avoided any close encounter with you for years. I wasn't supposed to be attracted to my husband's best friend. Part of me was ashamed I was."

Alex recovered enough to close the door. He remained in the entryway, though, arms folded across his chest, gaze narrowed as he tried to piece together her angle of approach. If she was out to prove how easily his body responded to her, she'd accomplished that mission. The way the damp, flimsy satin hugged her breasts had lust stirring to life. Her exposed skin wreaked havoc on his ability to focus. He ached to touch her again, to explore every inch of her delectable body until he had each curve, each valley, each unique little freckle memorized.

His head swam as her words conjured vivid images of the previous night. The sweetness of her scent as he lapped between her legs. The catlike way she arched her back, silently demanding more. Desire surged through his system like fire put to sagebrush, and he pulled in a deep, fortifying breath. The subject had to change before he forgot why he'd come inside. "Reagan—"

"This isn't *wrong*, Alex. Last night was everything I imagined...and more. I dare you to tell me it wasn't incredible for you."

"I..." He couldn't. It had been amazing. And the traitorous part of his soul that didn't give a damn about guilt, honor, or loyalty wanted her splayed out beneath him all over again. Right fucking now.

"That's what I thought." She gave him a sad smile. "Can't we just pretend for a little while?"

Like a stupid fish, he opened and shut his mouth. Twice. Just like that, she short-circuited his brain. *Pretend*. Could he just enjoy her, no strings attached, no questions asked?

He didn't want to know the answer—he suspected he could all too easily. Instead, he grabbed at logic like a drowning man thrown a life preserver. "What happened here, Reagan?" He swept an arm around the room, indicating the sad house. "Where did the insurance policy go? Where is Drew's family, and why aren't they helping? Where's Shelley?"

She shook her head, and her gaze clouded for a heart-beat. Slowly, carefully, she answered, "Shelley's been busy. I haven't had time to really talk with her." The touch of sorrow left her eyes as her tone became more decisive. "The man you knew wasn't the man I married. Can we leave it at that? Can that be enough for you?" She rose from the chair, crossed the distance between them, and stopped at arm's reach. Reaching behind her back, she unclasped her bra and dropped it to the floor. "Can *I* be enough for you… for a little while?"

A groan slid from his throat. Jesus—she expected him to think rationally when every temptation he'd ever craved stood right in front of him. *Offering* herself.

She didn't give him a chance to answer. She took a step forward and ran her fingertips down his chest. Alex backed up. If she touched him again, he'd crack into pieces.

Reagan followed his retreat, the subtle sway of her hips mesmerizing him. "Can it, Alex?" she whispered. "Or do we let life pass us by and regret it forever?"

She moved forward another inch, and her breasts brushed his chest. Even through the fabric of his shirt, her nipples were hard. The contact obliterated him. In one hot pulse of arousal, all that mattered was sinking home inside her, feeling her heat grip him tight, and reliving the ecstasy that she alone provoked. He was fucking addicted already, and God help him, he'd gladly go to hell for sacrificing his honor.

"No regrets," he murmured, dragging his gaze down her body, then back to her eyes.

He grabbed her around the waist, fused his mouth to hers, and spun her around so her back pressed against the wall. Bracing one arm above her head, he sank his body into hers. His hard cock pressed into her center, and he flexed his hips, stroking them both as he broke the hungry kiss.

Reagan's breath came out in a shaky exhale. She laid her head back against the wall. Eyes closed, she slid her hands up his chest, over his shoulders, and twined them around his neck. She levered her body against his, rubbing against his groin.

Another groan rumbled in his chest, and he dropped his mouth to the exposed vein on the side of her neck. It throbbed hard beneath his tongue. Her skin was cool to the touch, damp from her hair, and the scent of coconuts made him think of beaches, sand, and heat. Incredible heat.

Fuck, she felt like heaven. Tasted like heaven. How the hell did she do this to him so easily? He was putty in her hands...and goddamn, he didn't care. He couldn't get enough of the way she made him feel. He'd felt dead for so long. But every fucking time she touched him, she breathed life into his veins.

Yet, he didn't dare hold on to the hope it could go somewhere, that when all the truths came out, they had some sort of future. She refused to acknowledge what would always lie between them. When he pushed, she used passion to her advantage. He'd be foolish for thinking this was anything more than another means of avoiding grief.

But he didn't need permanent. He could do this without mixing it up. And he damn sure craved that pleasure. Craved her.

"I don't want to go slow," he whispered against her throat. "I want you hard and fast. I want to fuck until it hurts, Reagan. Can *that* be enough for *you*?"

She opened her eyes slowly. Desire turned those pretty blues a deep indigo. "Upstairs?"

In the bed she'd shared with…oh no, that was pushing things too far. "Takes too long to get there." He set his hands on her waist to guide her. "Turn around."

"No."

Alex blinked. He hadn't expected that.

She held his gaze steadily. "I want to look at you. I want to *watch* you take me."

A low growl slipped free as he hoisted her into his arms and headed for the couch. "There's not going to be much to watch if you keep talking that way."

A teasing grin spread across her delectable mouth and flashed in her eyes. "You wanted hard and fast."

"Oh, yeah." He laid her on the couch, then stepped back to shuck his clothes. With a nod at her, he indicated her shorts. "Lose those."

She didn't hesitate as she shimmied out of the shorts. She'd worn nothing beneath, and the sight of her fully naked on the couch stole the air from his lungs. For a moment, he stared, drinking her in. He'd wondered last night. Created a dozen fantasies. But nothing he'd ever imagined compared to the beauty of Reagan in the flesh. Her belly was flat. The slight flare of her hips was made for a man's hands, *his* hands. Toned thighs, sweet slender legs, and shapely calves.

His cock jumped against his abdomen, and a bead of moisture rolled down the shaft.

Reagan's gaze locked on his erection. She drew her bottom lip between her teeth, then released it and ran her tongue over it.

Desire gripped Alex so hard he nearly stumbled. But

she'd started this game, and he wasn't about to let her best him so easily. *Hard and fast.* If he held on to that thought, he couldn't get tangled up in emotion.

"I want your mouth on me, Reagan." His voice was coarse even to his own ears.

Her gaze lifted, challenge glinting in her eyes. "Where?"

"You know where."

She raised an eyebrow. "Let me make sure I'm clear. You want my mouth on your cock?"

Oh, God, she was killing him. His erection bobbed again, his body anticipating the wet heat of her tongue. "Yeah," he rasped.

"Maybe you should come a little closer."

Alex straddled her, his knees on either side of her ribs. She lifted her head, and the tip of his cock brushed against her lips. Her breath washed over his skin, coiling his entire body into a fierce knot.

When she parted her lips and closed them around the first inch of his erection, pleasure surged through his veins. He gasped, hard, and clenched one fist on the back of the couch. Closing his eyes, he focused on breathing as her talented little tongue worked around the ridge of his swollen head.

She leaned forward more, taking him deeper. An involuntary tremor raced down his spine as he held himself back from thrusting into the depths of her mouth. Choking her would bring this exquisite torment to an immediate end.

As if she sensed his building need to bury himself in her wet heat, she slid her hands over his ass and urged him forward. His body shook as he pushed in slowly. Savoring each incredible inch she allowed him.

When he reached the back of her mouth, her lips tightened around him and the pressure of her suck increased. He pulled back against the friction, then dipped back in. Her eyes closed, the corners crinkling as if she were truly enjoying herself.

Likely she was—she couldn't be immune to the shaking of his thighs as the thin tethers to his restraint threatened to snap.

He repeated the stroke again, and again, until he glided smoothly, his system on autopilot, chasing one drop of ecstasy after another. Sliding deeper into her throat with each painfully perfect thrust.

Pleasure ratcheted up until he thought he might implode if he didn't come. As release threatened to overtake him, he pulled out, sliding between her slick lips with a quiet *pop*, and hovered over her, panting, desperately trying to chain his desire.

"What's the matter?" she asked, wide eyes full of confusion.

"I'm not coming in your mouth," he managed between ragged gasps.

"What if I didn't object?"

It was all he could do to not groan. But as much as the idea of losing himself to her amazing mouth appealed, he wanted her body sheathed around him even more. He shook his head. "I want to hear you scream when you come. You can't if your mouth is occupied."

"I'm going to scream?" She raised both eyebrows, false innocence giving her expression a playful light.

Alex shifted down her body, nudging her thighs apart with his knees. She parted her legs farther, giving him a glimpse of the damp flesh between her legs. He groaned again, already craving her heady flavor. He was going to visit that soft skin again. Lap at it until she thrashed and begged for release. But not now. Now he was sticking to their agreement. *Hard and fast.*

He gripped his shaft, aligned it with her, and in one hard thrust, he sank home. Reagan let out a sharp cry and wrapped her legs around him tight. He eased back, braced his hands on her knees, and spread them apart. His gaze dipped between their bodies as he slid inside her again.

When he looked up and found her watching as well, his body bucked involuntarily. It was erotic as hell. Her watching him possess her. Focused on the way he pumped in and out of her body. Her breathing becoming sharper with each hard, deft stroke.

He felt the clench of her muscles. She tensed, widening her legs more, giving him room to slam home. And he couldn't stop himself if he wanted.

He pistoned in and out of her like a well-oiled machine, each hard thrust jostling her on the couch. She let out a soft, pleasured cry each time he hit her clit, pleasure clearly spiking through her as it consumed him.

With one last stroke, she shattered beneath him and thrashed her head as she let out the promised scream. Ecstasy rained down on his shoulders, carrying him into blissful oblivion. He surrendered to all-consuming release with a guttural shout.

Chapter Ten

Reagan dragged her nails up Alex's back and smiled. She loved how he felt against her, how he filled up all the empty places, including those deep inside. He fit like a glove. An expensive, supple leather glove made especially for her.

She turned her face toward his and pressed a soft kiss to his damp temple. She'd lost the courage that urged her to confront him half naked, but the truths she conceded were far more powerful. For now, she wanted to bask in the moment, in the all-consuming reality of him.

He blew out a hard breath as he adjusted his weight and braced himself on his elbows. With one hand, he stroked her cheek.

"You're priceless, Reagan," he whispered.

Funny how, when it was just the two of them, when they let go completely, he forgot all his objections. At times like this, the tenderness in his eyes made her think they might have a chance. That nothing would ever make him turn away from her. Not even the destructive truth. And the consideration he showed when they made love erased the thread of concern that he shared the same controlling nature as Drew. Her husband certainly hadn't shown restraint when it came to his sexual needs. Not the way Alex held himself back, waiting for her encouragement, seeking to fulfill her pleasure as well as his own.

He pushed off her, grimacing as he eased out of her depths.

She dropped her hands to his toned buttocks and held him in place. "Don't. Not yet."

"If you insist." Levering himself into her arms, he pushed back inside her body.

Reagan chuckled. Trailing one hand through his short hair, she grinned up at him. "Oh, I insist." Lifting up, she brushed her lips across his. "And I think you should do that again."

His eyes widened a bit, before a naughty smirk danced on his mouth. "You mean this?" Slowly, deliciously, he pulled out by a small fraction and then nudged back in.

Tingles spread through her body. "Oh, yes. That. Exactly that." Deep inside, she felt the stiffening of his cock again.

"Hm. I think I'm fond of that, too." He dipped his head, caught her earlobe between his teeth, and tugged gently. "Or maybe I'm just fond of you."

Another warm wave of pleasure flowed through her veins at his whisper. There was a deeper level of emotion to his words, one Reagan longed to believe in, longed to hold close forever. But there was no use focusing on anything but the here and now, so she held tight to what she'd been allowed and lifted her hips a tiny degree, creating the barest amount of friction.

Alex closed his eyes and drew in a long, deep breath, his expression tender. When he looked at her again, he set his strong hands on both sides of her head and stroked the hair at her temples with his thumbs. His hips barely moving, he gazed into her eyes and exhaled heavily. "I thought I could ignore how much I want you. And part of me wants to. But a bigger part of me is worn out from the fight."

She spanned her hands along his rib cage, then wrapped her arms around him in a snug embrace. It was a mighty confession from an honorable man, and the significance wasn't lost on her. "We don't have to make promises, Alex." *It's better if we don't.* Then he couldn't break them.

He nodded. For several minutes, he said nothing at all. The power of his forest green eyes held her captive. The intimacy of the silence made her heart drum heavily. And the slow, rhythmic motion of his body stoked a deeper, more engulfing passion.

Alex's serious expression gave way to a teasing grin, and he nipped the tip of her nose with his teeth. "I think we can agree to this promise." He pushed his weight onto his hands and leaned back, sliding from within her. Rocking forward, he thrust in again, hot, slick, and fully erect.

The slow, deliberate stroke brought Reagan's back off the cushions. She moaned as he filled her to capacity, stretching her tight, dragging himself over her G-spot. When he had sunk as far as he could go, he stilled, humor still glittering in his eyes.

"Well?" he asked.

"*God,* yes." She curled her nails into the tight muscle at the small of his back and rotated her hips.

He chuckled softly. "Do you have any idea how pretty

you are when you're aroused?"

At the simple compliment, heat filled her cheeks. She lowered her lashes, unaccustomed to the praise. For so long her life had been nothing but faults, errors, mistakes, and wrongdoings. Now, she simply didn't know how to react. *He can't be like Drew.*

Alex took the response out of her hands and drew her into a hungry kiss. The stubble on his chin chafed pleasantly. She drank in the taste of him, reveled in the erotic tangle of their tongues, until he tore his mouth away to suck in a ragged breath.

Closing his eyes once more, he increased their tempo, driving into her more steadily, more deliciously. Each time he pulled away, nearly withdrawing completely, she wanted to beg him not to stop. But just as the words rose to her throat, he impaled her again, stealing her air and making it impossible to speak. She clung to him, falling deeper and deeper into the man she'd always yearned for with every tip of his pelvis, every clench of his muscles.

Pleasure didn't just rise to envelope her, it hit like a jagged strike of lightning and was every bit as powerful. She bucked forward, crashing into his muscular chest as a sharp cry broke free. Alex crushed her close with a sudden sharp gasp, and his body tightened like stone. Deep within, she felt his release pulsing in time with hers.

He relaxed with a low, hoarse groan and lowered them both into the couch once more. "Jesus," he murmured with no small degree of surprise. "Didn't see that coming."

Reagan let out a light laugh. "Me, either."

He nuzzled the side of her neck. "I think you broke me." Amusement rumbled in his chest.

"Me?" She gave his bare buttocks a scolding slap. "That was all your fault, Alex McCray."

With a playful growl, he bit her on the shoulder. "Absolutely not."

"Uh-huh. I suppose—"

A light rap on her front door cut her off. She gave Alex a quizzical look.

He shrugged, his expression just as startled and confused. But he rolled to the side, giving her room to escape the couch. She grabbed his shirt and slipped it over her head as she sat, handily hiding her back. After her shower earlier, she'd meant to tell him everything—before she'd lost her nerve and changed the context of why she'd been waiting in the front room half naked.

Still tugging on her shorts, and feeling fairly decent as his shirt hung to her thighs, she went to the door and peeked out the window.

Desi stood on the other side, looking uneasy.

Reagan opened the door. "Desi? Is something wrong?"

"Ah, no." Color raced to her cheeks. "I walked by the window...um...I don't mean to interrupt."

Oh. *Oh.* Reagan's eyes widened. Behind her, Alex coughed as understanding evidently hit him, too. That must have been quite a shock to the unsuspecting. With the front window wide open, Desi had a front-row seat to an X-rated show.

Reagan choked down a laugh. "We're good."

"I'd say so." Desi smirked. She bent around Reagan, presumably to steal a glance at Alex. "Chance and I have steaks. He's firing up the grill. You two want to join us?" She waited a beat, gave Reagan a knowing look, and added, "Or would you rather…stay in?"

Reagan looked over her shoulder at Alex, who'd managed to drag on his boxer briefs and sat on the edge of the couch, clearly uncomfortable. His gaze held hers, uncertainty flickering in his eyes. She didn't want to push him into something awkward, but she could use the time in mixed company. The last hour or so had wrecked her, and her head was entirely too preoccupied with foggy, dreamy hopes of an unrealistic future.

Alex shrugged and then reclined on the couch with a sigh.

Up to her, huh? Well, the time in a relaxed environment, free from any pressures they could put upon themselves, would do them both good. She turned back to Desi. "How soon?"

"He's just lighting the grill. Say…fifteen minutes?"

Not much time to get cleaned up. Way too little time for conversation, however, and the last thing Reagan wanted was opportunity for Alex's head to get in the way of what they'd just shared. She gave Desi a nod. "Give us twenty, and we'll be right there."

Desi cast one more surreptitious look at Alex before tossing Reagan a wink. "See you in a few." She carefully picked her way off the porch, then turned and disappeared across the yard.

Reagan drew in a sharp breath, preparing herself for Alex to try to drag them into a discussion now that he'd had time to his thoughts, and turned to face him. But instead of serious introspection, or some frown of self-condemnation, he gave her a warm smile and beckoned her to the couch.

When she stood in front of him, his knees bracing both sides of hers, he set his hands on her waist and pulled her forward to place a kiss on her abdomen. "Thank you."

She slid her short nails through his hair. "For?"

"A little bit of normal." He caught the lightweight cotton fabric between his teeth, playfully tugged, then set her aside and stood. "I'm going to shower."

Dodging the suggestion that reflected in his gaze, she turned to pull the couch cover off the sofa. "I'll throw this in the wash and clean up in a few."

Not giving him time to comment further, she scooted from the room.

• • •

Alex dragged a fluffy towel down his shaven face and huffed out a hard breath. He stared at his reflection, searching for wisdom. Or maybe for courage—he wasn't entirely sure. Desi and Chance had been regular fixtures in Drew's life, and in turn, Alex had struck up a friendship as well. They were fun, they were smart, and Chance was probably the only person who lost at Monopoly more than Alex. But they'd accepted him as Drew's best friend.

Now he was sleeping with Drew's widow. What the hell would they think?

The change in his relationship with Reagan left Alex teetering on a ledge of uncertainty. If he stopped to consider it long enough, he'd think himself back into the rules box. But something had shifted inside him as he barreled headlong into orgasm. What had begun as something strictly physical, hard and fast to satisfy an urge, had transformed into something he couldn't put to words. But the part of him that had fought so violently against it now wanted to stand up and fight *for her*. To be seen as the man worthy of replacing Drew, to those who knew Reagan, but even more in Reagan's eyes as well.

But could he? Or would he always be the one who *hadn't* sacrificed himself?

He tossed the towel aside and plucked the tags from his new clothes. This had to be the strangest damn situation he'd ever gotten himself into. What was it she'd said? They didn't need to make promises? That was probably sound logic. Just go where the path led, until it eventually led them apart, and it would, when she realized he held the blame for the mess her life had become. He'd failed his best friend, and he would, inevitably, fail her as well. He just wasn't cut from the same cloth as Drew.

Everything else aside, he couldn't stay in Colton. Certainly not in a house that was void of everything that meant anything to him. Highly doubtful she'd leave—her best friends were here, not to mention her job, which she adored.

Frowning, he dragged on his clothes. He definitely didn't need to be questioning any of that. In fact, he was going to stop thinking all together. Every time he tried, it only cinched him into knots.

No, he was going to follow her suggestion and let *her* be enough for now. And he'd have fun tonight with two people he considered his friends as well. No more thinking, no more analyzing. No more punishing himself. There were steaks to be eaten, beers to be drunk, and if he knew Desi, some fantastic dessert to die for.

Yeah, it was odd stepping into Drew's shoes, but for this one evening, he was going to *make* it okay. If it required every bit of internal strength he possessed.

Chapter Eleven

As Reagan passed Desi a stack of dessert plates, she looked out Desi's sliding glass door, observing Alex. He relaxed in the patio chair, one knee casually tossed over the other, sweating beer in the closest hand, as he laughed with Chance. "He looks at ease for the first time since he showed up at my front door." Much more than that, he seemed *happy*.

Desi grinned as she slid a piece of cherry-covered cheesecake onto the top plate, then took it off the stack and set it aside. "He looks satisfied."

"Yeah, well." Reagan ducked to hide her blush.

"And so do you." She relieved Reagan of another cheesecake-laden plate. "I haven't seen you glow like that in a *long* time."

"I'm not glowing." With a roll of her eyes, she plucked a cherry off the top of the uncut pie and popped it into her mouth.

"You are." She dished out the last of the dessert, set the

pie server aside, and leaned back against the countertop, ankles crossed. "So how'd he take it?"

Mid-chew, Reagan froze. She should have known better than to hope the subject wouldn't crop up.

Desi's eyes widened in disbelief. "You haven't told him?" she asked in a hushed whisper.

"I...no."

"Why the hell not?"

With a heartfelt sigh, Reagan turned to the sink and began to absently pick at the dish towel. "I can't do that to him. He all but idolizes Drew. Telling him would be selfish."

Desi frowned sharply. "He probably feels guilty."

"He does."

A strangled sound of frustration gurgled in her friend's throat. "Then tell him, for God's sake."

She chewed on her lower lip, then confessed the deep, humiliating truth. "I'm afraid he won't believe. That he'll react like Shelley. Like Drew's whole damn family."

"Won't believe?" Desi stared, her mouth slightly agape. "You wear the proof. Shelley never saw the scars—you didn't have them then. He hadn't gone that far. Jesus, Reagan, you can't deny that kind of proof. Stop being afraid and take a chance. He's perfect for you."

In that moment, her hesitation had little to do with her own fear. More important was doing anything to protect Alex from the horrible truth of his best friend. Reagan shook her head and looked her best friend in the eye. "It's not that simple. It would crumble his whole foundation. *Everything* changes then, and I'm not going to hurt him that way."

"So you'd rather let him feel guilty. How generous of you."

Frustration rose. Desi didn't get it. She hadn't been standing in Reagan's living room to witness the anguish on Alex's face. Hadn't heard the fierce loyalty. She'd never been part of the military, couldn't possibly understand that brothers-in-arms were as tight as brothers-in-blood, if not more so. Telling Alex that Drew was an abuser would be like telling a sibling his brother was a pedophile. The truth would devastate him.

"Look at the tattoo on his arm, Desi—'Death before Dishonor.' That's Alex's moral composition." She raked her hands through her hair and let out a soul-deep sigh. "The man he owes his life to was a dishonorable man. You and I both know Alex well enough to know what that will do to him." She shook her head again, more convinced than ever that hiding the truth from Alex was the best way. Even if she couldn't maintain the charade forever. "I can't. I *won't*. Now, please, we're in a good place tonight. Let me stay there."

Desi held Reagan's gaze silently, then folded her into a tight hug. "I just want you to be happy."

"I know." Reagan embraced her just as tightly. "It's far from perfect, but I'm happier than I've been in years. And he's not staying long-term. So it's okay for now."

"If you say so." She backed out of the hug and gestured at the waiting desserts. "We better take these out before the guys come looking for us."

Reagan picked up two plates and headed for the screen door. Alex turned at the slight squeak to the hinges. A broad smile lit up his ruggedly handsome face as his gaze fell on her, making her stomach flutter. She took him his plate, feeling like she was walking on air.

To her complete surprise, as he accepted the proffered

cheesecake, he rose slightly from his chair and brushed a kiss across her lips. "Thank you, sweetheart."

From the corner of her vision, Reagan caught the look Desi and Chance exchanged—a knowing, supportive smile. They liked him. They liked him *with her*. And God how she wished Drew's ghost would stay in the grave.

"You're welcome." She resumed her seat beside him, leaning her knee against his. It was natural and comfortable, and in all the years she'd been married, she'd never felt so completely at ease.

• • •

Good food, good times…and one damned good woman. Alex squeezed Reagan's hand affectionately. He gazed out over the gas fire in a faux stone pit, seeing the picture the night presented from a distant perspective. Chance and Desi debated the legitimacy of Chance's long workdays with animated passion. Neither really caring which side they argued, just a strongly bonded couple poking good-naturedly at each other. At Desi's claim it was the only way he could justify three trips to Starbucks in a day, Chance burst out laughing and conceded the argument.

Beside Alex, Reagan sat in the chair, her long strawberry hair glinting with streaks of gold from the firelight. She'd shucked her sandals after finishing Desi's mouthwatering dessert, and her bare feet were tucked beneath her in the comfortable cushion. Sleep crept up on her. The heaviness to her sooty eyelashes, the lazy smile she couldn't quite make stretch all the way, and the occasional stifled yawn gave her exhaustion away.

Not that he could blame her. Today had been full of emotional highs and lows. Add in working on the roof, two bouts of sex, and no time to sneak in a nap, and he was feeling it also. But he was too content to do what he ought to and take her home so she could go to sleep.

Chance and Desi had embraced him like old times. Maybe even more welcoming than old times. Then again, that might be his wishful thinking, and he didn't trust the perception. But there was no reservation in their friendliness, no awkward glances, no stretched silences. And when Alex had been brave enough to kiss Reagan in front of them, he couldn't be certain, but he'd have sworn he saw approval reflected in Chance's face.

Maybe Reagan was right. Drew was dead; they hadn't stopped living. Maybe, despite everything, it would be okay to step into Drew's shadow. He wasn't the man Drew had been — would never be. But perhaps this entire clusterfuck was all in his mind.

Another round of laughter pulled him out of his head. Chance toasted Alex, evidently something he'd missed. He raised his nearly empty beer and then finished it off.

"'Nother?" Chance asked.

"I'm good. Thanks." He nudged Reagan's forearm. "You need anything?"

She blinked sleepily and shook her head.

"A bed," Desi said. "What did you do to her today, Alex? She's falling asleep in the chair."

He chuckled, grinned, but didn't answer. Desi knew; he was pretty damn certain Chance did also. Grinning, he tipped his head to study Reagan. Her blue eyes were luminous in the flickering light. Full of affection.

His chest tightened at that brimming emotion. She was tumbling over the edge, falling into him. Into *them*. And Christ almighty, he wanted to fall right along with her.

But could he? Could he let go enough to live? Could what they had right now be enough to make up for losing her in the end, once she realized he wasn't half the man she thought he was? Even more importantly, could they work through the past to make it through the future?

Or would taking the chance shatter him completely?

He lifted her knuckles to his lips. "I think she's right. To bed with you."

Reagan chuckled, but even her laughter had dimmed. As Alex's granddad would have said—she was plumb tuckered out.

He stood, tugging her to her feet alongside him. When she leaned into his side, he wrapped an arm around her waist. "Thanks for dinner, you two. It was great catching up again."

Chance rose and shook Alex's hand. "Vacation kicks in tomorrow. I'll lend you a hand with that roof, if you want."

"That'd be great. Thanks."

"Any time." Chance released Alex's hand, stepping aside to give his wife some room.

Desi hugged first Alex and then Reagan. "Glad you joined us. Night, you two."

"Night, Des." Reagan lifted her fingers to her mouth to cover a yawn.

Alex squeezed her close, then slipped his palm to the small of her waist and guided her to the screened-in porch door. The night was cool; the chirp of crickets added to the tranquillity. Stars twinkled overhead, a million tiny lights that lit up the crisp green grass.

She rested her head against him as they walked, her slower steps one more indicator that she was seconds away from passing out. In a strange, surreal way, it was nice, though. The trust she placed in him, the easy way she accepted him—he soaked it all in.

She made him feel normal. Special even, in a way he didn't deserve. God, how he'd like to be the man she believed he was. To be truly worthy of the tenderness he'd glimpsed in her eyes throughout the night. But he was just a man. Just an ordinary guy who put his pants on the same as any other.

Maybe that's good enough.

He reached her front porch and swallowed through the sudden ache behind his ribs. Who was he kidding? She'd buried a Purple Heart awardee. Even if she could somehow forgive him for his fateful decision, he'd never be the honorable man Drew had been. Drew fought the good fight till the end. Alex sure hadn't been the one to throw himself on a live grenade. Drew had dragged himself up from a life of near poverty. Alex came from wealth, had rarely had to work for much of anything in his teenage years. Drew wanted to become someone special, busted tail intending to become an officer.

Alex just wanted to be happy. Live a normal life. No notoriety. He'd served his country with all he was, but now he wanted a nine-to-five job that he could leave behind at the end of the day and go home to the wife he'd grow old and wrinkled with. Watch the kids play on the lawn.

Still…he couldn't tear himself away. Reagan had set claws in his heart, and though losing her would tear him apart, he couldn't stop.

She turned into his arms as he pushed open the door and leaned back to look up at him. "Stay with me tonight."

He kissed her on the nose. "What would you say to my sticking around a while?" Nudging the door shut with his heel, he stepped back to let her go to bed. "I like working with my hands, you need the help…" An excuse to spend more time with her. But damn, desperation gnawed at him. One more day. Just a little more of the bliss that made him forget.

• • •

Excitement burst behind Reagan's ribs. Alex here. Daily. For however long. It was like a dream come true. And at the same time, it was terrifying. She couldn't keep the truth from him forever. The longer he stayed, the sooner it would come out. Not to mention, she still suffered a degree of discomfort with his taking charge of her home repairs. If he wrote her out of the decisions…she couldn't deal with that again. Wouldn't.

But excitement overruled fear, and she swallowed to gain some control over her immediate impulse—to throw her arms around him and squeal in delight. "I think I'd like that."

"My sister's planning a surprise birthday party for me on Saturday. I'm not supposed to know about it, but my niece let it slip. Other than that, my time is yours." He paused a minute, chewing on the inside of his cheek. "You want to come with me?"

She blinked. Hang out with his family? Maybe there was more to his offer to stay than she realized. "Sure," she whispered.

He brushed his mouth across hers, drawing her into a lingering kiss. He tasted like beer and something far more delicious that was only Alex. Something darkly erotic she couldn't get enough of. The tangle of his tongue sent shivers of delight coursing through her body. The way he held her—securely and yet gently. Like a treasure he didn't want to break. She gave in with a murmur of satisfaction and let her body sway into his.

Alex drew the kiss to a reluctant close. Hands on her hips, he eased her away to arm's distance. "You should get some sleep, sweetheart."

Sweetheart—he'd started calling her that tonight. And the invitation to the picnic—could there really be more growing between them than just physical pleasure? Could he be sliding down the slippery slope alongside her? She tucked her fingers into his belt loops and pulled him back. "Sleep beside me."

The way his expression washed of all emotion set off sharp sirens of warning in her head. She watched his face, afraid to blink, certain whatever he said next would leave her in a broken mess.

"Ah…" He bit the inside of his cheek, pausing. "I can't sleep where Drew did, Reagan."

Oh, that. Relieved beyond all measure, she tucked her hand into his and started for the stairs. "You aren't. He never spent a night in my bed."

Alex came to a standstill, dragging her to a halt. "What did you just say?"

Reagan peered at him in confusion, then her eyes widened as she realized how he'd taken her offhand remark.

Her stomach knotted. She couldn't easily recover from that little slip. Time for more truth. Enough to throw him off the scent of her slip in speech. Just no details. Nothing too incriminating.

"The only time I slept in the master bedroom was when Drew was home. And then…it was never a full night. My bed's in the guest room." She'd go to her grave before she confessed that sometimes she'd been afraid she might not wake up if she spent the entire night with Drew. Never knowing what might set him off or what he would deem as proper punishment made self-preservation necessary.

Alex's face scrunched, his confusion evidently deepening. She swallowed down a groan. *Way to make it worse.*

"What?" he asked again, incredulous.

She tugged him closer to the stairs. Scrambling for a way to diffuse the rapidly deteriorating discussion, she blurted the first thing that came to mind. "I couldn't sleep through his snoring."

Visible relief flooded Alex's expression, and the tension in his arm faded. He snugged their hands together more securely. "In that case, I'll make you a deal."

She climbed another stair, taking him with her. "What kind of deal?"

"I'll share your bed if you promise to sleep. I refuse to feel guilty all day tomorrow for keeping you up all night."

Though she was too exhausted to even entertain the idea of sex, she sent him a coy, sideways glance. "I could sleep in."

He gave her bottom a playful swat. "I could sleep on the couch."

Reagan let out a laugh. "Okay, okay, you win."

Grinning, she led him up the stairs and into the room

that was her sanctuary. The room Drew had entered only once, and never again after she'd threatened to go to the police if he walked through the door a second time. That would have had him reporting to his commanding officer, which would have led to a formal citation, and given that she had visible cuts on her body, disciplinary action. To keep his record spotless, he'd never challenged her.

Alex led her to the bed, and then released her hand to strip out of his clothes. Momentary panic flittered through her as she realized she'd have to at least change. Thinking quickly, she opened the walk-in closet door and shut herself inside. She stripped out of her fitted T-shirt and jeans shorts and slid into an old, ragged shirt with a frayed hem and a pair of cotton sleep shorts.

Not very sexy but a necessity. If he asked, she'd remind him they were here for sleeping—at his insistence.

She exited the closet to find him stretched out in her bed. For a moment, the sight of his strong, powerful chest peeking out from the sheets rendered her motionless. With the moonlight pouring through the window, his skin held a slight ethereal quality that had her wanting to pinch herself to ensure the vision wasn't a dream. He dominated the full-size bed. *Her* bed.

The sudden reality that she was about to spend the entire night in Alex McCray's arms crashed into her, overpowering and overwhelming. Never once had she believed this could happen. But he was here now, he was real, and all the years of pain and misery were *finally* behind her. Hot tears welled in her eyes.

"Reagan, if you keep looking at me like that, sleeping will be taken off the table." He rolled onto his side and patted the empty pillow. "We'll have to renegotiate."

Caught in the act of staring, she jerked to attention and scrambled to the opposite side of the bed. She slid beneath the covers and snuggled up to him with her head on his shoulder. Indulging in the freedom to at last touch all she wanted, she smoothed a hand down the centerline of his chest, across his abdomen, then laid it over his heart.

He covered her hand with his as his lips danced through her hair. "Sweet dreams, Reagan."

"Only of you." Closing her eyes, she tucked her leg between his.

Chapter Twelve

Sunlight streamed in through Reagan's open window, urging Alex to get up and join the day. He woke to the sweet smell of coconut and Reagan's long hair draped over his pillow. Smoothing one hand down her rib cage and over the flare of her hip, he fought the stirrings of desire all over again. Sound asleep, she was even more beautiful than awake. Softer. Somehow more vulnerable, which evoked a fierce protectiveness inside him. She deserved so much better than was her current lot.

Leaning toward her, he pressed a kiss to her soft cheek. His cock stirred as she shifted position and her bottom brushed against his groin. But her lack of response only reminded him how exhausted she'd been the night before, and he choked down lust. Later, he'd indulge. When she was already awake.

He took care to not disturb her, slipped out of the comfortable bed, and dragged on his clothes. If he was going to stick around a bit longer, he'd need to go to an actual cloth-ing store—these were clean enough for today, but he'd only picked up the bare minimum. And he sure as hell wasn't go-ing to ask her to do his damned laundry.

Alex took another long look at her, memorizing the way the pillows engulfed her delicate body, and then headed to the door. As he reached for the knob, an unsettling feeling descended on his shoulders. She'd said something last night. He couldn't put his finger on what it was, exactly, now, but the niggling awareness something wasn't right tugged at his mind.

"Ghosts," he muttered as he stepped into the hall and quietly pulled her door shut behind him. He was letting ghosts interfere with a perfectly beautiful morning. *Not going to happen.*

His gaze strayed to the master bedroom. Unease pulled at his gut. *Go away, Drew. Today is mine.* And maybe tomor-row. And the next day. And the next—until Reagan came to her senses and realized he'd never be the hero her husband had been.

Grinding his teeth as the feeling of inadequacy rose again, he determined not to let it get the best of him. He had a roof to finish and a porch to get started on.

Damn, the house was already filling with heat. Today would be a scorcher. But Saturday drew closer, and he want-ed the exterior fixed by then so he could relax completely.

He'd really asked her to attend the picnic. He probably ought to alert his sister. Though she'd have a dozen ques-tions he didn't want to answer. Still…an idea came to mind. He could do something nice for Reagan, something that might help her out a little. She needed support he couldn't give. Particularly given what he knew of Drew's death and how his family had seemingly abandoned her.

He stopped in the kitchen, pulled out his phone, and dialed.

His sister answered on the second ring. "Hey, little man."

Alex chuckled at the age-old nickname. "Hey, Red. So, about this supposed family picnic Saturday."

"Supposed? There's nothing supposed about it."

"Right." He smirked. "You know it's a birthday party. I know it's a birthday party. Don't worry, I'll act surprised." He wouldn't rat out his adorable niece for spilling the secret.

Diane grumbled on the other end.

Before she could offer an objection, he asked, "Did you invite Shelley and her folks?" The sorrow in Reagan's eyes when she relayed she hadn't had much time with the sister who had been like her own surfaced in his memory.

"Uh…"

He glanced out the back window, picturing the last time Shelley, her husband Aaron, Drew, and Alex had barbecued around the grill. Reagan and Shelley had been as close as thieves. Shelley could help where Alex couldn't, he felt certain. It would do her good to have time with her. "I'll take that as a no?"

"Well, I don't have a number for her, and I didn't want to go through Drew's parents—you know Mom doesn't like his mother at all. It would be rude to not invite them."

"I've got her number. Call her, would you? I think Reagan would benefit from seeing her."

"Reagan? You're bringing her?" Surprise colored Diane's question.

"Might as well." He did his best to downplay the

situation. "She's by herself now, you know."

"Uh, yeah, I know. And I know how you used to talk about her."

Damn, he hadn't expected that. Had it been so obvious? Had Drew seen anything? He frowned. Did it matter, really, now that Drew was gone? Reagan had put it aptly—they hadn't died with him. "Look, I care about her, obviously. And we have strong bonds between us. She's buried in a lot of shit, and good friends would bring a bit of unexpected cheer. So use all that energy you were storing up to surprise me and direct it her way."

His sister, with her ever-burning need to help others, grabbed on to the suggestion and giggled like a kid in a candy store. "Oh, that's so thoughtful. We could make it like a homecoming party, only for Reagan. A big show of support."

Yeah. The more she talked, the more he liked the idea. Do something nice for Reagan. Something to bring her out of her sorrow. If it helped her confront the reality—well, she needed to *grieve*. And he'd be right there for her. "Sounds good, Diane. Thanks."

"Okay. I'll get right on it. Give me her number."

Alex rattled off Shelley's number, and after a bit more discussion on what Reagan's favorite snacks were, he terminated the call. Now, to tackle the other issue looming over her shoulders—her house.

He found a magnet notepad hanging on her fridge and scrawled a quick note that he was heading to the lumberyard again. After leaving the note prominently affixed to her countertop, he slid on his shoes and let himself out of the house.

A quick glance at the rickety front porch promised it

wouldn't be a simple repair job. The floor was sound enough, but the overhang had taken so much damage it had fully collapsed on the far end. Overhead beams splintered at various angles, breaking at their individual weak points. One had crashed into the door—presumably the one that compromised the door's hinges—and had been propped in the corner where the porch recessed at the entrance to the house.

He picked his way through the growing rubble and moved closer to the destroyed corner, eyeing the exterior wall of the house where the crooked shutter dangled. Yes, indeed, she had duct tape over the glass—the whole upper right-hand corner was nothing but. Evidently covering a sizable hole or crack. *Miracle the whole thing didn't shatter.* Then again, he'd seen storms do some crazy things. Amazing how Mother Nature could be deadly yet as gentle as a lamb all in the same instant.

Dread rolled around in his belly as his gaze skipped to the eave and the corner of the roof where he'd been working. The siding buckled like a giant had stepped on the top. Exactly where the tree had fallen.

Alex sighed. Don had been right—her house had taken structural damage. He might fix the damn leaky roof, but it was going to take an expert to put her house back together correctly. No sense in going to the lumberyard. The whole porch would have to come off.

Where the hell is her insurance company?

He'd ask later. She'd implied she didn't have the deductible. But that didn't answer the questions about Drew's life insurance policy and his death benefits. And Alex was pretty damn certain someone could help her out after the appropriate loops had been navigated.

In the meantime...

He glanced around again, taking in the poor home that had once been picture-perfect. She was living like a freaking pauper, and it bothered him down deep in his soul. He couldn't excuse it. Couldn't justify it. And he damn sure wasn't going to allow it to continue. They'd work out financials when her insurance company came through. And if not...well, it wasn't like he had anyone else depending on him or his money. He certainly wasn't going to use it. Not the substantial amount he'd accumulated as a bachelor with very few personal needs the marines hadn't provided.

Footsteps inside drew his focus back to the window. He caught Reagan's shadow as she approached the front door. She stepped out, then stopped, startled.

"I thought you were at the lumberyard."

Alex grinned at her disheveled hair and the raggedy T-shirt she wore. He hadn't noticed the fraying hem or the hole at the collar last night. On her, worn as it was, it looked cute. The mini sleeping shorts she'd donned before crawling into bed brushed the tops of her thighs—damn, how the hell had he missed that this morning? It was a waiting playground for his fingers. Not to mention an irresistible tease.

"Change of plans," he said, clearing away the direction of his thoughts with a short cough. "This porch has to come off before it can be fixed." No sense breaking the bad news that she was in for one hell of a repair to her home. He didn't want to spoil the day with the first words out of his mouth.

"Oh." Her surprise faded, and she gave him a narrowed gaze as she leaned against the doorframe. "So you're going to cut it off?"

"Yep. Chance offered to help. I'm going to take him up

on it."

"You two didn't mention it to me."

Her voice held an edge he couldn't interpret. He cocked his head, confusion tugging at him. "It's rather obvious it needs extensive repairs."

"Well, yes, but it's my broken porch. I should be involved."

Chuckling, Alex crossed to her and kissed the tip of her nose. "It's demolition, baby doll. There's no real decision-making involved. You were there last night when he offered to help. When we put it back together, you can input all you want. Promise. Now…" He reached into his back pocket, withdrew his wallet, then pulled out his credit card. "You have an AC guy?"

"Yes, why? It can't be fixed. It has to be replaced." The edge in her tone had lessened but still lingered.

Determined to eradicate it completely, he nodded, his smile broadening. He'd never really *helped* someone before, and the idea of helping *her* made his heart light. He passed her the card. "Go see them in person. Get someone here today to replace the compressor."

When she hesitated, her gaze locked on his credit card, he bounced his hand, urging her to take it. Drew's voice echoed in his memory. *Had to take away the credit card before she broke us completely.*

Alex shoved the memory aside, along with her hesitancy. He murmured, "I have plans for you tonight, and they don't involve involuntary sweat."

• • •

Reagan blinked hard. Alex was offering his *card*. In all of her marriage, Drew had never set her free with any of their credit cards. Not even to fill her car up with gas. Hell, he rarely gave her cash. If she wanted something, it either came out of her salary or he had to purchase it—and not without a great deal of resistance.

As Alex pushed the card a little closer, she hesitantly took it out of his fingers. A whole new sense of elation rushed through her, and she gave him an equally uncertain smile. "Are you absolutely sure?"

He shrugged. "I've saved well. It's just a little money. And if I'm sticking around a while, I don't want to be miserable indoors. It's already heating up, and it's only ten."

She nodded again, stunned by both his generosity and the unhesitating way he granted her access to his money. He trusted her. She wouldn't let him think she'd take advantage of him—she'd bring him the receipt. Then he'd know he hadn't made a bad decision. Nor would he doubt her or wait around for the statement to come.

"Pick up some wine while you're out?"

"Wine?" she echoed, once again, caught off guard.

Giving her a sexy grin that made his eyes dance, he nodded and gestured at his card. "Get your favorite, whatever it is. I told you I have plans for you tonight."

A shiver stole over her, the promise in his words unmistakable. His resistance had faded, and she didn't quite know what to make of the man who stood before her, insisting she spend his money, no longer arguing about Drew or what they shouldn't be doing. Her heart skipped three beats before it kick-started hard. He was *accepting* them.

His "plans" suddenly had her weak in the knees. She

cleared her throat as warmth flooded her body, and she reached for the door. "I need to get dressed, then I'll go." As an afterthought, she offered him his card back. "Want to hang onto it till I'm ready?"

Alex brushed her question off with a nonchalant wave of his hand. "No need. I'm going up." He nodded at the roof. "Got a few more shingles to put in place, then I'll see if Chance is up and about."

Dumbfounded, Reagan made her way indoors. So this was what it felt like to have a man's trust—who would have known it could be so…fulfilling. But damn, would that make telling him the truth more difficult? Would he feel like she'd betrayed him?

Of course he will. You're deliberately keeping something important from him.

Frowning, she trudged up the stairs. Yes, she was keeping secrets. But not for her benefit. Question was, would he realize she was trying to protect him?

Likely not. Which meant she didn't dare get caught up in the fantasy of Alex. Because she couldn't keep him. And she damn sure wasn't going to be the person who shattered his illusions. He'd seen enough horrors of mankind; he deserved some innocence.

But if she wasn't careful, the truth would slip out some-how. She'd saved the conversation last night, but who knew when he might casually mention something and she flubbed it up by not thinking through before she spoke.

The only other option was to convince Alex to leave. And she would if it meant saving him from the monster Drew had become. She'd tell him their budding relationship was meaningless, that it had come to its natural end, and she'd break her own heart to save his.

Thankfully, that time hadn't come yet. She could still enjoy him for a little while. And right now, she had a compressor to replace—a *loan* she'd repay as soon as her next paycheck came. The next month would be tough on her budget with the added expense. She'd have to mind every penny and live on bare essentials. But she refused to leave Alex room to think she'd taken advantage of him.

Feeling a little more in control of the speeding train she'd somehow climbed aboard, Reagan quickly changed, ran a brush through her hair, then tugged on a ball cap. Compressor, wine, and a night of Alex. The best gifts a woman could have.

Chapter Thirteen

"Need a hand?"

One arm wrapped around the porch's cracked corner post, Alex looked down from where he stood on the ladder. He lowered the pry bar in his opposite hand to his side and chuckled at Chance. "It's about time you joined the land of the living. Desi said you were still asleep an hour ago."

Chance shrugged and picked up a broken two-by-four Alex had removed earlier. "What good is a hot tub if you never use it?"

"Uh-huh. Just like what good is a twelve-pack if you never drink it?"

A wide grin split his face. "Exactly." He gestured at the crushed roofline level with Alex's head. "What's the plan?"

"Tear it off." He frowned as he surveyed the sunken-in overhang. "Without blocking the front door." A task he had yet to figure out how to accomplish. Particularly with only his two hands. The support beams ran the full length of the porch roof. Cutting one in half would only compromise the standing part of the roof, directly over where Reagan entered her house. Once he removed the last of the support with the beam he currently balanced against, the stability would be dicey, at best.

Chance dragged a branch out of the rubble. It shifted beneath Alex precariously. "I spent a summer on a rough-in crew," he said as he casually tossed the log aside. "Firewood." He reached again, grabbing a large hunk of what had been the porch roof. "Anyway. If we can get to the cross beam, we can cut it off there. Leave the main support on the outside edge. That should hold her."

"What are you doing?" Alex gestured at the debris he tossed to the side.

"Looking for something to use as a brace."

Alex climbed down from the ladder with a slight frown. "All this is just…crushed. That tree fell and *wham*. Nothing left." He pushed aside bits of shingles and wood with the toe of his boot. "Drew used to keep lumber in the woodworking shop, but Reagan's moved all that."

Chance nodded. "Yeah, she wants to turn that into a greenhouse. Had a plan and everything until this." He indicated the mess in front of them with a sweep of his hand. "If that asshole contractor she hired ever shows his face again, I'm going to strangle him."

A strange sense of jealousy spread behind Alex's ribs. Chance was one of Reagan's closest friends, and it was natural for him to look out for her. But Alex couldn't shake the instinctual protest that the contractor who'd boldly taken advantage of her was *his* to strangle. That Chance felt the same protective instincts as he did only unsettled him more.

He didn't like it. Didn't like the idea of some other guy taking care of her. Even if that guy was one of his own friends. He nodded, stifling a response.

Chance stepped off the remains of the porch and pointed toward the former woodshed. "See the fruit trees out there?"

Alex nodded again.

"The greenhouse was supposed to stop just shy of them. She wanted a range and storage unit in the existing shed. So she could harvest the apples, walk just a few paces instead of all the way to the house, and can out there." He flashed Alex a grin and chuckled. "She always misses the peaches—damned deer come up from the trees. Thought she might be able to ripen them up if she picked them early."

Alex frowned as the same sense of unease he'd experienced that morning crept over him again. "I don't get it, Chance. Maybe you can explain it to me."

"What? The greenhouse?"

"No. There's *nothing* left of Drew in the house, and it's not like he's been gone for years. Don at the hardware store has more to say about him than she does."

Something passed across Chance's expression, a look that resembled what Alex had witnessed too many times in the field—that of a man who'd seen something he wanted to forget but couldn't. It passed just as quickly, replaced by another chuckle. "Let me guess, Don went on about Drew being a hero? Get used to it—the whole town holds him in reverence. Half the people here think Reagan didn't deserve him. Don't believe everything you hear."

His offhand remark only served to add discomfort to Alex's confusion about Reagan's behavior. He frowned and looked away, turning back toward the porch. "He said his wife disapproved of Reagan selling Drew's tools."

"His wife doesn't approve of a lot of things." He chuckled softly. "Don's a good guy, though. Did he invite you to the VFW?"

"Yeah. Said he and the boys would give me a hero's welcome."

Chance joined Alex on the porch, his amicable smile back in place. "You should take him up on it. Those old boys have the market cornered on top-shelf scotch and vodka."

Alex shook his head. "I'm not a hero, Chance. Never was, never will be. And it's pretty damn awkward trying to explain that to everyone."

Chance picked up the pry bar and applied it to a loose section of roof. With a jerk, he pulled loose worthless nails and sent another chunk tumbling onto the pile of debris. "Sure you are. What do you think you're doing here, with this roof, this house?"

Blinking, Alex stared at Chance. "Helping out a friend."

Chance gave him a pointed look. "You're not friends."

Alex's frown deepened. "Sure we are."

With a short bark of laughter, Chance pried off another chunk of worthless wood and shingles and tossed it aside. "Whatever makes you comfortable, man. But I'm telling you, if you're sleeping in her bed, you're not friends."

Sleeping in her bed… The nagging feeling he'd fought throughout the day clanged into place. The statement Reagan had made the night before echoed in his head. *I couldn't sleep through his snoring.*

Son of a bitch—he'd slept near Drew for the last several years. Drew didn't snore. For that matter, he slept like a rock and damn near didn't move once he was out.

He stared at the rubble, unease churning in his gut. Why had she lied? Better yet, why hadn't she shared the bedroom with her husband?

"Alex?" Chance asked, eyebrows lifted.

"Hm?"

"I asked you to hold that post steady."

"Sorry." Pulling himself out of his mental fog, he supported the broken corner post. If they hadn't been sleeping together, and she'd packed up his things so quickly, maybe they'd had trouble in their marriage. An impending divorce certainly made the idea of being involved with Reagan more comfortable, but Drew hadn't mentioned problems at home.

Come to think of it, Drew rarely talked about home. Only the occasional mention he was calling Reagan, or she'd sent him something he'd needed. The exception being remarks about finances; he never talked problems—they'd always seemed exceedingly happy.

"Earth to McCray," Chance called with a touch of amusement. "Are you ready?"

"Yeah," he answered absently, securing his hold on the post.

Chance jerked hard on the pry bar, hard enough to make the broken roof shudder. The post Alex held on to shook under the duress, threatening to break clean in half. He steadied it as best he could as a four-foot section of overhang broke free from the foundation wall. It creaked unsteadily, supported only by the post Alex held and the intact section on the opposite end. If he let go, the entire thing would come crashing down and block the front door.

As Chance scrambled down from the ladder, picked

it up, then hauled it to a new position, Alex's focus turned inward again. If everything wasn't good in Drew's marriage, why in the world would he be concerned enough to ask Alex to look after Reagan?

"Hey, Chance?" he asked. Normally, he wouldn't resort to asking third parties. But in the few days he'd spent with Reagan, she'd made it exceedingly clear she didn't feel like discussing Drew—another hint that perhaps divorce had been in their immediate future.

"Yeah?" he answered as he mounted the ladder again, chainsaw in hand.

At that moment, Reagan's car pulled into the drive. Alex groaned inwardly. So much for getting answers. "Never mind," he mumbled.

Chance fired up the chainsaw and applied it to the dangling section of roof. Alex's concerns about the state of Reagan's marriage vanished as she strolled up the short walk and stopped at the porch steps. Her gaze caught his, mesmerizing blue pulling him in deeper than he wanted to fall. In the afternoon sunlight, her hair shone like strands of gold had been woven through the endless lengths. But her smile, the beguiling uptick of her lips that spoke of shared secrets and intimate promises they had yet to fulfill, made the space behind his ribs suddenly too tight. His entire body homed in on her presence. From head to toe, he ached to touch her.

She waved with the fingers of one hand then turned, cutting a path around the house, presumably to enter through the back door. His gaze fixed on the sway of her hips and the heart-shaped curve of her ass. He wanted that bottom up against him, flexing beneath his hands as he took her from behind. Wanted to see the muscles in her back tense as she pushed back against his cock.

He gritted his teeth and forced his attention back on the roof that now dangled on two corners. Chance killed the chainsaw and climbed down from the ladder. He nodded at the post Alex held.

"That corner next. Then it should pull right down flat. There's not enough tension to take the rest of it with her when she goes."

Alex took a half step sideways, allowing Chance room to climb on the debris pile and reach the top corner of the post.

One swipe of the chainsaw sent the shattered portion of the roof tumbling. A cloud of dust rose from the rubble, and with the weight no longer threatening the post, Alex let go to survey Chance's work. The foundation wall was clean. The front porch supports still remained—all of them solid and strong, save for the corner he'd supported. It would need to come out eventually. Along the crossbeam, Chance had cut far enough away that the intact portion of roof was mostly solid. But contrary to his belief it would hold entirely, several boards near the seam between porch and house jutted up and down at awkward angles, having been broken loose when the larger chunk fell. Those would need to be pulled out first thing tomorrow, before they could come crashing down on anyone's head.

But right now, he had air-conditioning to investigate. And one very fine ass waiting for him inside.

He shot Chance a look. "Thanks, man. I think I'm going to call it a day."

A smirk pulled at Chance's mouth. "Tell me again you're friends."

"Can it," Alex grumbled good-naturedly. "Gentlemen

never tell." Gentlemen also didn't consider the things he was thinking of doing to Reagan's body, but so be it.

Chance burst into laughter. Shaking his head, he hefted the ladder onto his shoulder and picked up the chainsaw. "I'll put these up and get out of your hair. Don't do anything I wouldn't."

Oh, he was planning on doing a whole lot of things that Chance better never even consider when it came to Reagan. But Alex nodded and gave him a wave. As Chance rounded the corner of the house, heading for the woodshed, Alex let himself in the rickety front door. He eyed the beam overhead, cringing inwardly as it teetered, barely balanced between two others. Yeah, that had to go. But it was too high to reach, and the ladder was now gone. He'd get it later this evening.

A thick cloud drifted in, blocking the sunlight. He glanced toward the horizon, noting building clouds. Another storm—good thing he'd patched the leaky roof. They could stay in tonight, get a reprieve from the heat with the incoming front, and weather the storm with wine and a whole lot less clothing.

He closed the door behind him and headed for the noises coming from the kitchen. Reagan stood at the counter, a stack of red potatoes piled up to her left. He approached behind her, wrapped his arms around her waist, and nuzzled the side of her neck. "Hey, you. I missed you."

• • •

Bliss blanketed Reagan as Alex's warm lips caressed her skin. She closed her eyes and leaned back into his strong arms, releasing the potato she held to the cutting board. Contentment purred in the back of her throat. "Missed you, too. Sorry I was gone so long—waited forever for an answer on the compressor. They can't come until tomorrow. Your credit card is in my purse. Let me get it."

The stubble on his chin scraped alongside her neck. "Hang on to it."

Hang on to it. It took a second to accept it really was that simple, that he wasn't concerned. "Looks like you and Chance got a lot done on the porch."

"We did. I called my sister, too, and told her you were coming Saturday. She's looking forward to meeting you."

Meeting her—that sounded so…intimate. "Really?" she asked as casually as she could.

"Yeah, really."

His hand drifted over her belly, up her ribs, and cupped her breast, sending automatic heat surging through her veins. As she shivered, he stepped closer, bringing her bottom into direct contact with his groin. Through their clothing, the hard evidence of his arousal pressed between her buttocks. She resisted the urge to grind into him.

"Damn," he murmured, his voice hoarse. "You should never be let out of the house wearing those shorts." He dragged his thumb across her nipple, and then kneaded the soft flesh of her breast.

Desire coiled her stomach into a tight knot. She shifted, her breathing becoming ragged. The cant of her hips rubbed against his erection, and Alex sucked in a sharp breath near the base of her ear. But beneath the pull of arousal, old fears stirred to life. Was he annoyed by her choice of clothing? Would she now pay for a mistake she hadn't realized she'd made? Would he, too, try to control her freedom, take away her choices?

As Alex's teeth grazed her collarbone and his other hand flattened against her belly, pressing her bottom more securely to his groin, she shoved hard at the ridiculous fear. This was Alex, not Drew—clearly, he *liked* her choice of dress. And he'd made it evident this morning, when he'd stressed she'd have input on the rebuilding of her porch, that he wouldn't make decisions for her.

He tipped his pelvis into hers, stroking her once more. "Come shower with me," he whispered. "I'm aching to put my hands all over you."

Shower…the idea nearly melted her into a puddle. What she'd give to lather his body, slide her hands all over his slickened skin. Lap off the water after he rinsed, drop by drop by drop. But it was nothing more than a fantasy—she would be fully exposed. In daylight. Where the obvious would be impossible to miss.

With a short, forced laugh she hoped sounded casual, she eased out of his embrace, turned, and planted a chaste kiss on his lips. "If I do that, then we won't have dinner."

Alex caught her around the waist and dragged her closer. Dipping his head, he flicked his tongue against the sensitive hollow beneath her ear. "I'm okay with starving. Really."

She laughed more genuinely. Playfully, she pushed at his chest. "I'm not, handsome." To soften any possible interpretation of rejection, she hooked her fingers through his belt loops and closed her hands, holding him in place. "Besides, I have it on good authority you'll need your energy later."

He arched an eyebrow. "I can think of a better caloric intake."

"No, that's burning calories, silly." She giggled, fascinated by this teasing side of him. He seemed so at ease. So content with their newfound intimacy.

"Mm. Pardon me. I can't seem to think straight with your hands so close to my cock." He captured her lips with his teeth, tugged, then released them to brush a soft kiss across her mouth.

Feeling playful herself, Reagan shifted one palm over his erection. "Better?"

Alex let out a groan. "Worse. Now I don't care about food at all." He flexed his hips, pushing against her hand.

She massaged him for a moment, reveling in the way he closed his eyes and parted his lips, stuttered breaths escaping. She'd forgotten the sheer delight that came with touching a man's body. Even when her marriage had been happy, she'd never experienced the unspoken power she wielded now. And that control humbled her as much as it thrilled her.

Alex opened his eyes, and his gaze scorched beneath her skin. "That countertop is looking pretty good right now."

Reagan grinned broadly, squeezed him tight, then slid her hand up his chest. "I cook on that countertop."

Alex smirked. "Hey, I'm not picky about where or when I taste you. If it's on the potatoes…" He shrugged.

Laughing once more, she pushed at his chest again. "Shoo. Go shower. I'll finish dinner, we can eat, and then, my dear, I'll put my hands wherever you want them."

With a growl, he tugged her close. "Promise?"

"Cross my heart."

He kissed her soundly, licking his way into her mouth and tangling his tongue with hers before breaking away with a protesting grunt. "Damn, you've got me hard as a rock."

"They say cold water helps," she answered with a smirk.

He smacked her on the butt before releasing her completely. "There are much, much more helpful things." Reaching around her, he snagged a baby carrot. "I'm pretty partial to warmth. Specifically from your mouth." He pointed the carrot at her. "You're in trouble for this, minx. The way I ache right now—you're so going to pay later."

Reagan jammed down the reminder of a similar threat with a drastically different meaning. But her smile faltered, and she turned back to the counter to mask any possible reflection on her face. With a forced chuckle, she replied, "Quid pro quo, Alex. Tit for tat."

"Definitely tit. Yours are perfect."

She turned around to give him a false glare.

"Okay, okay, you win. I'm showering." Grinning, he popped the carrot into his mouth, held his hands up in surrender, and backed toward the stairs. "If you change your mind…"

Struggling to maintain a straight face and failing miserably, she pointed the knife at him. "Out."

His laughter echoed up the stairs. Reagan placed the knife on the counter, braced her hands on the edge, and pulled in a deep breath. In the silence, the walls pressed in around her. She was falling for him, falling hard and fast. And the only thing that waited for her when she hit the ground was heartache. Devastating, complete heartache. Because no matter how she wished otherwise, the excuses wouldn't last much longer. He'd catch on to her evasion tactics. He'd ask questions. And God help her, she didn't know how to answer.

Chapter Fourteen

Alex reclined on the sofa, legs stretched out before him and propped on the table, ceiling fan swirling overhead. Reagan sat tucked against his side, her attention fixed on some television show he'd tuned out of long ago when the hot, sticky air had finally made it impossible to think of anything else. It was fucking miserable in this house, and the rainstorm that had blown through had done nothing to alleviate the unmoving humidity. Dinner and the oven only amped up the temperature.

Hell, it was even too hot for sex. And that was saying something, considering he'd been at half mast since he stepped out of the shower.

He disentangled his arm from around Reagan's shoulder and sat forward. "You know what sounds good?"

She blinked as if the sound of his voice had startled her. "Um. Why don't you tell me?"

"Ice cream." He stood, captured her wrist, and then

pulled her to her feet. "Mint chip ice cream. Let's go to the store." When she looked like she might balk, he tugged her close for a quick kiss. "It'll cool us off. And so will the air-conditioning in my truck."

"Mm. You don't want to do that. AC in the vehicle only makes coming back inside worse." She bent for the remote and flicked the television off. "Let's walk. There's a breeze out there, too. It's just not hitting the windows right."

Anything would be better than sitting here in the sauna. Alex headed for the door. "The repairman promised he'd come tomorrow, right?"

She nodded as she followed him outside. "He had to pick up the compressor from the warehouse tonight. He'll be here around nine."

Thank God. Alex closed his eyes to the subtle breeze as Reagan shut the door. It was definitely cooler outside, and the song of locusts was soothing against the lavender of twilight. He reached for Reagan's hand automatically. When her delicate fingers twined with his, he caught her sky-blue gaze. His heart stuttered for a minute. Sometimes it felt so damned natural it was frightening. He could almost convince himself they were stepping out of *their* house. That she belonged to him. That he could be the man she deserved.

Before melancholy could intrude on his contentment, he gave her fingers a squeeze, pulled himself out of the depths of her gaze, and led her off the porch. The beam overhead caught his attention again, and he made a mental note to secure it first thing in the morning.

They walked along quietly, her stride as casual as his, as if she, too, enjoyed simply being together. Alex soaked in the quaintness of Colton, the elderly couples watching the sunset on their front porch, dogs barking somewhere in the neighborhood, children playing not too far away as fireflies began to light up the shadowed yards. He'd never really paid much attention to the town. It was just another place, one he stopped in with his best friend before once more eating dust in the middle of some desert village half a world away. But now, he felt the charm as keenly as he felt Reagan's presence at his side.

And he liked it more than he'd ever dreamed he might. Chicago was loud and imposing compared to Colton. Impersonal. Cold in a way this little town could never be. Roots were set down here, meant to last and withstand the hands of time. Hell, the old man sweeping out his garage across the street had probably been born here as well.

"How'd you end up in Colton?" he asked as they approached the edge of town and made a right-hand turn down another block.

"The house was Drew's grandmother's. His father didn't want it when she passed shortly after we were married. I wanted four true seasons." She grinned at Alex. "Storms may have their downside, but I love the severe weather each spring and fall. And snow—I hadn't seen snow in years. Not since my grandparents took me skiing when I was little."

Ah, that's right—Drew's father had retired from Fort Benning the year before Drew married Reagan, then he'd moved his family closer to the lakes so he could follow his second passion—fishing. Drew had followed in his dad's footsteps, enlisting shortly after, though Alex had thought Drew intended to make the marines a career. He did the math in his head. "So you two moved here just before boot camp then?"

She nodded, swinging their hands between them as they walked. "Colton worked out well. I could attend the university for my degree, and we're close enough that when he finished his six years, he could commute to a job in Chicago."

Finish his six years? Alex frowned. "Wasn't he planning to re-enlist?"

Reagan nodded. "Yeah. Things changed from the initial plan."

There was something in her voice Alex couldn't put his finger on. Sadness? Likely because he was dragging her down memory lane again, bringing up the dreams she'd built with Drew. At least she was talking. But had she been building dreams? If they'd been heading for divorce, maybe what he detected was just sorrow over failed hopes. Divorce seemed a lot more plausible if she didn't intend to travel with Drew and wanted roots in Colton.

Not wanting to drag her into the past too deeply and destroy the inroads he'd achieved, he changed the subject. "If you could go anywhere, where would it be?"

She tipped her head, regarding him sideways, and grinned. "In the States or out?"

"Anywhere in the world."

"Easy. Venice. You?"

"I could do Venice." Hell, he could almost see her floating in a gondola, her head tipped back as she laughed, that musical melody carrying over the rippling water. His heart skipped again. Damn. He was falling for her fast. He needed to pull back now before he couldn't keep the lines separate any longer.

"But where do *you* want to go?" she asked as she led him down another turn, and the old storefronts rose up to greet them on both sides.

"Always wanted to see Africa. The Serengeti and all the wildlife. I was crazy about big cats as a kid."

"Oooh. That sounds better than Venice." Excitement filled her voice. "One of those Jeep tours through the brush? And oh! The giraffes!" She stopped like she was picturing it in her head, and then added, "And maybe a gorilla. They have gorilla nurseries there. We talk about it in my classroom. It'd be so priceless to hold a baby. But that's in the Congo."

"Congo is en route to Serengeti. We could do a couple days." He caught himself as the words slipped out. Was he really doing this? Building dreams with her like…like a couple? With a deep, steadying breath, he let go of the fear. *Just talk. No promises.* Not like it would lead to anything anyway.

The excitement in her voice increased. "I bet there are tours. Gorillas and lions appeal to a lot of people."

"The Virunga National Park has a gorilla rescue, and elephants, and lions—though the cats aren't like the Serengeti. And a volcano."

She flashed him a sweet, breathtaking smile. "You've really studied it, haven't you?"

He chuckled, momentarily self-conscious. "Yeah. I guess I have."

She drew them to a stop in front of a deep blue and white building with a small gathering of people crowded around the benches and tables—evidently half of Colton had the same urge to beat the heat with ice cream. As they approached the counter to place their order, she said, "Could still go down to the Serengeti. I wouldn't want to go to Africa without seeing the giraffes, after all. And you'd get the big cat excursion."

"It's doable. And surprisingly, not terribly expensive." He gestured at the menu board. "What are you in the mood for?"

Her eyes twinkled mischievously, and she dragged a slow, deliberate gaze over his body—leaving no mistake to her meaning. His muscles coiled tight. The desire he'd held at bay came surging to the surface. He dragged in a deep breath, fighting down the hunger, but held her twinkling gaze and allowed the energy to crackle between them.

A pretty flush crept into her cheeks, and she looked away, the hint of a smile lingering on her mouth. "Chocolate. Two scoops on a sugar cone."

Alex stepped forward to the counter, putting them in place behind a young couple with a small boy about five years old, who stood behind an elderly couple.

"Alex McCray, is that you?" a man asked from behind him.

He turned, surprised anyone in this town would recognize him enough to call him by name. Approaching quickly, a wide grin splitting his face, was one of Drew's friends, Jacob. He'd come to a couple patio parties when Alex had been in town. But otherwise, they barely knew each other.

"It is you." He thrust out his hand and shook Alex's vigorously. "I thought…I mean we all heard…" His gaze skirted to Reagan, and then shifted uneasily back to Alex. His exuberance dimmed. "Glad you made it through."

Alex blew out a hard breath through his nose. This discussion wasn't anywhere on his list of things he wanted to do tonight. But clearly, it was unavoidable. Anything he might say would only come off as rude. "Good to see you, too, Jacob."

The elderly couple filed off, two sundaes in hand. Alex said a quiet prayer that the family of three would order quickly and he might be spared from a drawn-out attempt at reminiscing.

No dice. Jacob gestured over his shoulder to a pretty brunette and a lanky boy who looked to be about twelve or thirteen. "Have you met my wife?"

"Don't think so."

Jacob gave Reagan another uneasy glance before addressing Alex again. "Come and say hello? I'd love to introduce you. And my boy would be over the moon if you'd say hi. He looked up to Drew, and his cousin just joined the air force. He'd be thrilled to shake your hand, you being a real war hero and all."

Alex's stomach churned. He was *not* a hero. Hell, the story everyone knew was nothing but a fabrication for the most part. It wouldn't have looked good to let it slip that they'd disobeyed orders to help two kids, thus putting the rest of the company in danger. Nor would it have looked good to proclaim the orders had been to *ignore* two innocent kids. So the higher-ups concocted something that sounded decent to the press. Surprise attack. Men fought valiantly. Good lives lost.

"If it's an inconvenience…" Jacob trailed off, evidently uncomfortable with Alex's prolonged silence.

Alex shook his head. With no good excuse to offer, he said, "No, it's okay. Just a minute." He withdrew his wallet from his back pocket, pulled out a twenty, and then handed it to Reagan. "Can you get our ice cream?"

She stared at his hand like she'd never seen a twenty before.

Alex arched an eyebrow. One hesitation to accept money from him he could write off to pride. But two? Over ice cream? The sixth sense that had kept him alive in the field began to buzz. His gaze narrowed as something dark and ugly flitted across his mind, but he couldn't quite put words to it.

Reagan pulled herself together and took the money out of his grasp. Her smile was shaky and nervous. "I'll bring you back the change."

Wasn't that kind of a given? He watched her for a second, and then nodded at Jacob, who was only too pleased to lead him over to the table on the north side of the elongated patio.

Spends like it's the last buck she'll ever see. Drew's half-chuckling tone echoed in Alex's memory. He'd been joking, hadn't he? Teasing when he'd said he'd locked her down?

Jacob stopped at the edge of his family's table. He lowered his voice and inclined his head where Reagan stood. "You two look pretty close."

Alex had enough years of his sister's attempts to nose in on his life to recognize fishing in an instant. Since he didn't intend to divulge, he ignored the observation.

It didn't work. Jacob gave him a grin. "Just keep an eye open. Fantastic teacher, but she's been *different* since Drew's death."

"Different how?" Alex's protective instincts rose, and a guarded edge slipped into his voice.

Jacob shrugged as his wife slipped a hand onto the small of his back. "No one's seen hide nor hair of Drew's family since his death, and they used to come by at least once a month. Don't you find that odd? And the way she sold all his stuff — or didn't you know?"

"Honey," his wife chimed in, "are you going to introduce me?"

Alex did his best to stop the frown that tugged at his brow and turned to shake the woman's outstretched hand. "Alex McCray. I served with Drew Sanders."

Whatever Jacob had been alluding to disappeared with his wife's exclamation of praise. She pulled their son out of conversation with a kid his age, and Alex found himself battling recognition he didn't want.

• • •

Reagan concentrated on breathing, one hundred percent aware of how she'd just behaved, what she'd let slip through. Not that she could help it — Drew had controlled her, then he was gone, and the money she'd spent since had been her own, not handed to her. Take the virtual imprisonment out of the equation, and she'd probably still feel weird accepting anyone's money.

But Alex had noticed. And she needed to get her shit under control before she backed herself into a corner she couldn't escape. Why the hell was her deceased husband coming back to haunt her so powerfully now, anyway? This morning, today in the kitchen, tonight…

Because she was falling for Alex, and Drew hadn't always been the asshole the marines turned him into? Because some stupid part of her brain was waiting for the monster inside Alex to emerge from the shadows?

"What can I get for you, Mrs. Sanders?" asked the teenage girl behind the wide glass window, a sibling of one of her students the previous year.

"Um." *Ugh, don't call me that.* She inhaled again, found a smile, and shoved everything else but ice cream aside. "Double scoop chocolate on a sugar cone and a double scoop of mint chip on a sugar cone. You're Brent Tippins's older sister, Lynette, right? How's he enjoying summer?"

"Oh, he's good. He and Dad are hiking in Colorado this week," she answered over her shoulder as she scooped out the ice cream. "Mom and I have the house to ourselves."

"Your parents doing okay then, too?"

She nodded with a smile, showing off a set of braces. "Yep. My aunt's getting married next week in Chicago, so Mom's been helping her a lot. Making flower arrangements."

"That sounds like fun." Reagan accepted the first cone.

They made small talk until Lynette had finished Alex's cone, and then Reagan turned to scan the tables. She found him ruffling the mop on Jacob's thirteen-year-old son's head, and her breath caught at the sight of him. He cut a powerful and strong figure. His short dark hair accented the chiseled lines of his profile and matched the faint stubble on his chin. Standing in the salmon light of an unforgettable sunset, he was as handsome as the first day she'd ever laid eyes on him. Maybe more so now that they'd formed their own special bond. Her heart sure beat a lot crazier now. But then, she didn't have to hide her reaction to him any longer. Didn't have to worry that if she smiled a bit too brightly or kept eye contact a second too long, she'd pay for her unwitting crimes.

Alex turned, his dark gaze locked with hers, and he excused himself from Jacob's family. As he made his way across the patio to join her, those green eyes shone with hungry intensity. Like he could devour her as easily as he intended to devour his ice cream. Warmth spread through her veins. He made her feel special. Like she was the only woman in the world he'd ever notice.

"Thanks," he murmured as he accepted his cone.

She thrust the change at him. "It was eight-seventy—" She stopped. There was no need to spell it out for him. If he was concerned, he'd ask, and he wouldn't *be* concerned.

As if driving her own logic home, he arched one eyebrow while he stuffed the money into his front pocket. But then, whatever suspicion he might have had faded as he licked the top scoop. Closing his eyes, he let out a soft, dramatic moan. "Cold."

She nudged him with her shoulder, chuckling. "Thinking of trying out for the community theater?"

He smirked. "Maybe. Always wanted to perform on stage." The teasing light in his eyes filled the statement with innuendo.

"Exhibitionist, huh?"

Taking her by the arm, he guided her to an empty table on the far corner of the patio. "Sweetheart, you could get me to do a lot of things. Hell, you have me on your roof. I don't do that for just everyone."

"Hm. Roof, huh? Now there's an idea." Suppressing a grin, she looked over the top of her cone, doing her best to hold on to a look she hoped came across as deadly serious.

He didn't buy it—rich, hearty laughter rumbled in his throat. He leaned his head back and gave in to it, and all the tension she'd felt at her stupid hesitation over a twenty-dollar bill vanished into the night.

Chapter Fifteen

Alex inhaled the sweet night air, breathing in distant flowers along with freshly cut grass as he walked alongside Reagan, heading for her home. The little excursion for ice cream proved to be just what he needed. Jacob's line of questioning turned out to be nothing but concern for Reagan, alleviating his worries and prompting him to invite Jacob to the surprise gathering as well. He also relayed that Shelley would be present and to extend the invitation to anyone Jacob thought Reagan might enjoy seeing.

The idea of bringing happiness to Reagan left him satisfied on a level he hadn't comprehended previously. Even more important, tonight he'd felt entirely at ease doing something simple with her, doing something *normal.* If it had been a date, after the initial weirdness with the money, it would have gone on record as perfect. He'd laughed. He'd flirted. He'd lost his damn hesitation and let the ordinary man out of the box...and she'd made him feel like he'd finally come home.

Every part of him was warm and happy. All the chaos of war erased from his mind. All the sorrow of losing his friends rubbed out by her.

He glanced up at the sky. The stars were out in full although the lack of a moon dimmed their light. The night air had cooled him off. Well…parts of him. The other parts waited in anticipation, anxious to shut the world away and strip off her loose black shorts and the simple gray T-shirt she'd spilled ice cream on. To devour her with his tongue like he'd done with his ice cream.

He popped the last of his cone into his mouth, licked the fingers on his left hand, and slid her a sideways glance. She looked up at him, a smile crinkling the corners of her eyes. Ice cream dotted the tip of her nose.

Alex burst out laughing.

Reagan blinked. "What?"

He tugged the hand he held so she was closer and brushed the chocolate dollop off with his index finger. "You're like a little kid. It's not good enough unless you wear it?" He let his gaze drop pointedly to the smear on her shirt, across the top of her left breast.

Another woman might have taken offense. Another woman, he wouldn't have dared tease. Reagan, however, punched him lightly in the shoulder, wrested out of his grasp, and rubbed the back of her hand over her nose. "Ice cream's one of those things you have to fully invest in to appreciate." She glanced down at her arm, frowned, then rubbed at a sticky smudge on the inside of her elbow.

"So good you have to bathe in it?" He smirked. "Next time, you get a cup, not a cone."

"Bathing in it might be fun." She waggled her eyebrows before pinning him with a false frown. "If my company wasn't so distracting, I might have better focus."

"Oh, it's my fault now?"

"It's always your fault. Those are the rules, don't you know?" Her mouth quirked as she fought off amusement.

Alex poked her in the ribs. Before he could spit out a witty remark, she squealed and ducked to the side.

That sound was guaranteed to turn a full-grown man into an obnoxious teenager. He lunged for her.

Reagan shot sideways, laughing as she scampered across the neighbor's yard. He pursued, chasing after her long strawberry hair, spurring her on faster. Good thing most of the block was dark—he probably looked like the kid trying to pull the little girl's pigtails.

Giggling, Reagan bolted beneath a thin, low-hanging tree branch. Too late, he realized she'd pushed it out of her way. It snapped back and lashed him across the chest. Not hard enough to hurt, but enough to throw his stride off. He stumbled for purchase, regained it quickly. But she gained wide-open ground and dashed across her front lawn.

He kicked it into high speed and reached her heels just as she hit the front porch. "Now you'll pay," he threatened amid chuckles. With one last burst of effort, he caught her by the wrist.

As he tugged on her to turn her around, she giggled again and jerked on the front door. Alex's humor ground to a stop as the overhead beam jostled loose. One end slid toward her head.

He thrust his free hand up to bat it away, seconds before it connected with her shoulder. Reagan's expression washed white. She recoiled as if she expected his reckless, hurried swat to connect with her face.

Alex froze. In the immediate and heavy silence, the board clattered to the front porch. *No.* He had to be imagining things. Those blue eyes absolutely were not filled with terror. They couldn't be.

She cleared her throat, straightened, and pushed a lock of hair out of her face. When she blinked, whatever he'd seen in her eyes disappeared. But her smile didn't return. She stepped inside the house, all traces of their play erased by a stiff demeanor.

His mind struggled to rationalize what he'd swear he'd just witnessed. It was natural for her to flinch—something was coming at her head. But she hadn't seen it. Hadn't noticed the board at all. Just his hand moving closer to her face.

Had someone hit her before? She'd married Drew young, didn't speak to her family. Was this why? Had her fucking father been an abuser? Rage churned deep in his chest, tightening his muscles so hard he ground his teeth together.

"Reagan." Alex stepped inside and shut the door behind him.

Before he could get another word out, she wrapped her arms around him and dragged him into a hungry kiss.

• • •

Just keep kissing him, and it will go away.

Reagan breathed through her nose, keeping her mouth fused to Alex's, afraid if she stopped to drag in air, his questions would break free. In that half second of stillness when she'd realized he had never intended to hit her, she'd read the curiosity in his eyes. The mix of disbelief and understanding.

Son of a bitch...what the hell was wrong with her? She'd reacted on instinct. She *knew* Alex McCray would never hurt her. Not intentionally, at least. She'd moved past this, so why did her brain have to skip out and ruin a perfect evening?

She moved her hands up Alex's corrugated chest, shutting off her brain and allowing herself to become lost in the greedy tangle of his tongue, the feel of his warm skin. What had happened on her doorstep was forgotten as his strong hands dipped over her bottom and squeezed, molding her against his body. His heart thumped hard beneath her fingertips. His breathing became labored.

The pressure in his fingers increased, biting into her buttocks as tension crept into his shoulders. She'd become familiar enough with his signs to know he was losing himself as well. Giving in to the desire that ignited every time they touched. As he tipped her pelvis into his, and she rubbed against the hard length of his cock, muted sounds of pleasure rumbled in the back of his throat. She curled her nails into his pectorals, aching need opening deep within.

"Alex." She pulled back, panting. "God, you drive me crazy."

He rested his forehead against hers, dragging in hard gulps of air. Eyes closed, he clenched his fingers once more in a hard grip that told her he clung to the edge of control. "I want you more than I've ever wanted anyone, Reagan."

That simple, hoarse statement went straight to her heart and melted it. She slid her hands down his chest, twined her fingers with his, and squeezed affectionately. "Make love to me in my bed. Please?"

At his slow nod, she turned toward the stairs. She tried not to hurry, tried not to let it show she was starved for his touch. But in the end, the twelve steps to her room became too much. She jogged the last few.

When they were inside with the door closed, Alex gathered her into his arms. He dragged his lips across hers, and then raked his teeth against the side of her neck. God, it was crazy how the littlest touch could make her feel like she was on fire. She slid both hands into his hair, pressing his mouth to her harder, tugging at the short strands as her knees threatened to give way.

"Kiss me," she rasped.

He flicked his tongue out, trailed lazy little circles, and slowly worked his way back to her mouth. But he didn't kiss her. He teased with fleeting little touches that were as soft as a butterfly's caress and drove her half out of her mind. If he'd just…stay…put.

Reagan groaned. "Please. I love the way you kiss me."

Alex brushed his mouth across hers once more, lingering longer as he whispered against her lips, "What's so special about my kiss?"

"It's like you're starved. Starved for me." Her voice lowered as embarrassment rose. Had she really admitted that? Did it sound too presumptuous? *Dear Lord, don't let him laugh.*

He didn't laugh. Nor did he sate her yearning by drawing her into that kiss.

He went utterly still, his shallow breath echoing in the room.

She squinted through the darkness to gauge his expression. What had she said wrong? Despite the shadows, she caught the movement of his Adam's apple as he swallowed.

"I am starved for you, Reagan," he confessed huskily. "I've been starved for five goddamn years. And if you were smart, you'd run like hell."

Confused, she searched his face for what he wasn't saying. "Why?"

He cupped a palm around the back of her head and drew his hand slowly down her hair, guiding her cheek to his shoulder. Like he didn't want her looking at him as he spoke. "Because every time I touch you, I want more. And if we keep on like this, I'm going to want your goddamn heart."

That did it—as if her body were molten wax, her knees buckled, and she crumpled into him. Only the fierce hold she maintained on his shoulders kept her from falling completely.

It's already yours. The thought stopped on the tip of her tongue. She wanted to say it. *Yearned* to tell him. But doing so would cross a line they didn't dare breach until he knew everything.

Alex lifted her up and carried her to the bed. He set a knee on the mattress, laying her down gently as he lowered his body over hers. When he gazed into her eyes, emotion scalded into her, so hot, so raw, so everything she'd ever dreamed of.

"Do you want me still, Reagan? Knowing that?"

She framed his face between her palms and licked her lips. His gaze tracked the motion of her tongue, and the muscles on the edge of his jaw ticked. Did she dare say yes, knowing she might break him into pieces?

"I do." The confession tumbled out breathlessly, beyond her control. Her heart was in charge now, and it didn't give a damn about logic. It wanted him. Wanted to *belong* to him in every way possible. Body and soul.

With a throaty groan, Alex claimed her in a hot, ferocious kiss. His tongue delved deep, possessing her from the inside out. Stroking so perfectly the ache between her legs became painful. She shifted beneath the weight of his body, rubbing against the hard length trapped behind his fly just to find a little relief.

Shaking his head, Alex broke off the kiss. "Not without me."

He reared back on his knees and reached for the fastener to her shorts. One deft twist of his wrist popped the button free. In seconds, he had both shorts and panties in a pile on the floor. The very air, still as it was, scraped across her nerve endings, and she whimpered, lifting her hips, in dire need of full body contact. Now.

Alex smoothed a rough hand down the top of her thigh. "Easy, sweetheart. Give me a second."

As she nodded, he slipped off the bed and made quick work of his own clothes. Exquisitely naked, he rejoined her on the bed, kneeling between her calves, running his hands up and down the outside of her legs. "Open for me," he whispered.

She complied, unhesitatingly.

He shimmied toward the foot of the mattress, then stretched out, lowering his head. His breath dusted across the juncture of her legs, the heat almost too much to bear. She bit down on her lower lip and tensed, certain if he put his mouth on her, she'd come apart at the barest touch.

But she didn't. When Alex dipped his tongue between the wet folds of her sex and licked her slowly, she didn't shatter in his hands. Instead, the gnawing hunger deepened even more. She arched her back, pressing into the slick slide of his tongue, twisting her head against the intense pleasure.

He slid one finger inside as his mouth found her clit. In…out…in… He thrust slowly and steadily, all the while stroking the sensitive little nub until she writhed from the pleasure of it all. "Alex, please…oh…don't stop."

Her inner walls contracted with a sharp burst of ecstasy…that fell short as Alex stilled. He lifted his head, watching her as she gulped in sharp breaths, her entire body shuddering. Denied the fulfillment she craved, she let out a soft moan.

When her body relaxed, he repeated the whole process over again, slowly building her up, bringing her to the critical point, and then backing off completely. Then he waited, only to do it all over once more. Driving her wild with desire. She snatched at his shoulders, dug her nails in hard, twisting her head side to side. Reagan cried out something but was so lost to sensation she didn't know what she said. Just sounds wafted through her awareness. Pitiful little sounds that had to be begging him for more.

"Fuck, Reagan," he whispered against the top of her thigh. "Do you have any idea how beautiful you are? Even with that goddamn shirt on." Rising over her, he gripped the hem and tugged the shirt over her head, leaving her in just her plain white bra. He tossed it on the pillow beside them. "Much better."

"Alex, *God,* I need…"

In the dim light, she saw him nod as he braced his hands

on either side of her shoulders and levered his body into hers. "I know what you need, sweetheart. I do, too." He flexed his hips, slipping the tip of his swollen cock into her wet flesh, still taunting her with the promise of release. She parted her legs as far as she could, desperately trying to draw him deep inside where the ache burned like fire.

"*Alex*," she moaned.

He nudged the barest bit of him inside her opening. "See what you did to me in the kitchen earlier? Paybacks are hell."

Jesus, how could he possibly be thinking of paybacks when she was going to die if she didn't come? She slid her hands around his ribs and scraped her nails down his back, lifting into the heat of his body. "Please don't do this," she choked out. "I…please…"

A gravelly chuckle escaped him seconds before he fused them together with a kiss. As his tongue stroked hers, he pushed deep inside, filling her completely. Her inner muscles contracted around his cock, guiding him deeper as she undulated beneath him again. When he'd sunk as deep as he could go, a groan vibrated in his chest. His body shuddered, and he tore his mouth away to suck in an unsteady breath.

Then, whatever game of torment he'd begun came to an end. He guided one of her legs up and hooked her ankle over his shoulder. Bracing his weight on one arm, he leaned into her again, shifting higher so that each thrust put his body in contact with her clit. She cried out with each sharp burst of pleasure, each deep purposeful stroke. His mouth found hers again, swallowing the sounds she couldn't hold in.

Ecstasy rose and engulfed them both at the same time. Reagan felt it consume her, felt it drag her so deeply into

Alex she couldn't define where he started and where she began. Felt it connect her in a way she had never connected to anyone.

And she was terrified. For in that instant, she knew Alex McCray held something Drew never had—he held the power to shatter her. Not with fists, not with bruises, but with love. The kind of love that could destroy her if she lost him.

Alex rubbed his cheek against hers, then dusted his mouth across her lips. Slowly, he freed her leg and eased it onto the bed. Then he collapsed on top of her, his cheek nestled between her breasts, one hand roaming aimlessly along the side of her ribs.

Afraid of what she'd just discovered within herself, Reagan hesitantly ran her hand down his back. *I love you, Alex. I love you so much.*

"Am I too heavy?" he asked.

"No, you're just right."

"Mm. That was…incredible. *You* are incredible." He nuzzled her breast with his scratchy chin as he eased himself out of her and rolled to the side. "I'm going to pass out. Fair warning."

She curled into his arms, breathing in the scent of his skin, and closed her eyes. There was no one like him in the world. No one else who had the power to make her feel cherished, to make her feel like she was worthy of the fierce emotion that glinted in his eyes. No one else who could erase the scars.

She pressed a soft kiss over his steadily drumming heart. "Good night, Alex. Sleep tight."

He mumbled something unintelligible, and then his breathing evened out. She waited until his embrace turned leaden, then nudged his arm. When he didn't move, she eased out of his hold, dragged on her shirt, and lay back down. As she turned onto her side, tears threatened. It had become inevitable—she had to tell him. Because if she didn't, they could never have a future. And yet, telling him was the one thing likely to drive them apart.

Chapter Sixteen

Alex woke with a start, momentarily unaware of his surroundings. Sweat dampened his chest, and though he couldn't recall what he'd been dreaming of precisely, he could feel the nightmare clinging to the fringes of his mind. He didn't often revisit the horrific day Drew died, but every now and then, when stress piled on, it haunted him in sleep.

He squinted at the bright light shining through the window, his heartbeat still not quite right, and eased a leg to the floor. Sitting upright, he cast a glance over his shoulder at Reagan, who lay sound asleep, one delicate hand tucked beneath her cheek, blissfully unaware he'd been fighting demons in the dark. Probably best she didn't know. He wasn't yet ready to tear what they had apart with the truth and have her discover he was nothing but a fraud. Tomorrow, they had the party, and to be honest, he looked forward to it too much to muck things up beforehand. She would be so happy to see Shelley, and bringing her that brief happiness, amid all the crap she was going through, gave him a sense of satisfaction.

Quietly as he could, he slid out of bed and tugged on his boxers and jeans. There was something inherently wrong with the fact that his body was more sated than he could ever remember it being, and yet, he couldn't relax enough to enjoy the comfort of a warm, soft woman sprawled across the bed next to him. But damned if he could shake the unsettling feeling clinging to his shoulders. It was like watching a horror flick—he knew something waited at the top of the stairs.

And somehow, it all began with that terrified look in Reagan's eyes last night.

He trudged down the stairs to the kitchen and started the coffeepot. Normally, he wasn't a coffee drinker. But after only a handful of hours of sleep, he could use the caffeine boost. With it already going on nine, and the repairman due any minute, he needed to wake the hell up. He leaned against the counter as he gazed out at the backyard.

Somebody hit her.

While the coffeepot brewed, he clenched a fist on the counter. He didn't want the thought to be true, but no matter how he tried, he couldn't come up with a different explanation for why she would have looked so scared when she hadn't seen the board slipping toward her head.

She'd been perfectly happy. Normal. Carefree. Playing and laughing. Then *bam*! A one-eighty out of the blue.

When the coffeepot gurgled into finish, he stuffed a mug under it and filled it nearly to the rim. Cradling it between both hands, he went outside to think.

The minute he stepped onto the front porch, another

memory flared to life. That of Reagan's hesitation when he'd handed her his credit card. Then again at the ice cream shop. Looking back, comparing them side by side, he could see it wasn't a matter of pride. Hell, she'd almost seemed… dogmatic about the way she started to count back his change.

Like she'd been…

His fingers clenched tighter around the cup.

Oppressed.

Alex ground his teeth together. Her defensiveness about being included in decisions; the way she avoided talking about Drew— *No.* It simply wasn't possible. Drew wasn't a douche bag. For fuck's sake, he'd saved a three-legged puppy over in Afghanistan, let alone the two boys and Alex. Guys who did that didn't come home and beat their wives. Besides, Drew adored Reagan. That's why Alex was here in the first place.

Look after Reagan. Drew's voice echoed in Alex's head.

His attention wavered from the gory memory of holding his best friend's bloody hand as a long gray van pulled into the drive. A pudgy guy with a buzz cut climbed out and waved.

Alex lifted his mug. "Morning." He glanced down at his attire—jeans still partially unfastened, bare feet, no shirt; there could be no mistaking the nature of his involvement with Reagan. Not that he was trying to hide it. Half of him just expected someone to call him out with the truth. That he was poaching Drew's widow.

Fuck, what was the matter with him? Yesterday, he'd been content with things. Now, he was back in the funk. Unable to shake a really bad mood that was coming on strong.

Who the fuck hit her?

It had to be her father. She'd *fled* her family. He could think of no other explanation. *Bastard.*

The guy in the drive opened up the back of the van. With the help of a dolly, he unloaded a compressor unit. The slam of the doors was like a gunshot in the quiet neighborhood, and Alex flinched. He was already crabby; he didn't need loud noises to start his morning off. But if he wanted the thermostat to read something other than "sweltering," he'd have to grin and bear it.

Maybe not grin. He grunted something he hoped was welcoming as the man approached, the dolly parked at the base of the porch. "Mind if I come in and kill the breakers?"

"Come on inside." Alex held open the door. "Might keep it down, if you can. Reagan is still sleeping."

The man's face split with a wide grin. "You must be Alex?"

Alex arched an eyebrow.

He indicated his clipboard. "Work order has your name on it. Jacob's my friend. Grew up together." He stuffed his hand out to shake. "Ron James. Pleased to meet you. Heard you were over there with Sanders."

"I was," he answered more gruffly than he intended.

Using the clipboard, he tapped his left leg. "Bum knee kept me from basic. Otherwise, I'd have put my time in, too. We need more of you around here in Colton. Give these kids someone to look up to and learn from."

Alex clenched his jaw. "You wanted that breaker box?"

At Alex's gruff tone, Ron's expression blanked, then with a blink, he nodded. More subdued, he answered, "Yeah. If you don't mind."

With a nod, Alex ushered him through the door and down to the basement. When he'd shown the guy the box, he left him to his work, set his unfinished coffee in the kitchen, and then went outside to deal with the damned broken boards above the front door. He might as well do something useful. Maybe keeping active would keep his mind from blowing a few untimely oddities from Reagan out of proportion.

• • •

Three hours later, Alex had managed to tear a gaping hole in the good roof, smash his thumb in the process, and drop two boards on his foot. All because he couldn't concentrate. His mind simply wouldn't leave the incident last night alone.

Along with doing more damage than help on the porch, he'd managed to catalog every reason why this thing between Reagan and him couldn't work. Including the undeniable fact that she hadn't grieved the past enough to move forward.

As another board he hadn't intended broke loose, he tossed the hammer onto the porch with a muffled oath. Enough of that shit. He'd end up having to demolish the entire structure at this rate. He was hot, sore, and pissy. He wanted air-conditioning and a shower. But instead of pronouncing that the repairs were all complete, Ron had only brought more bad news while Reagan was still sleeping. A relay and the central switchboard in her inside unit were fried. Likely, they'd taken some sort of power surge when the lightning hit that fucking tree. She didn't just need a new compressor. She needed a whole new unit, inside and out.

Not wanting to wake her, Alex took the initiative to set her up with a top-of-the-line system, regardless of expense. Still, it would be close to five before they'd have air. *If* Ron could track down the unit today. He'd left thirty minutes ago, exactly ten minutes before Reagan stumbled out of bed. Alex hadn't ventured down from the roof to tell her before now—he hadn't wanted to infect her with his bad mood. Unfortunately, his annoyance wasn't fading, and she'd want to know why her house wasn't cooling down. He needed to chill before he tackled that conversation. She'd likely be annoyed over his making decisions for her.

He jerked the front door open, stalked past where Reagan sat in the front room, and into the kitchen for something cold to drink.

"Everything okay?" she asked.

Alex tugged on the refrigerator door and stuck his head inside. "No," he snapped.

"What can I do?" In the corner of his vision, she appeared just behind him, reaching for the fridge door. "Let me get you something. Did you eat anything this morning?"

Grimacing, he swallowed another short remark. It wasn't her fault he was in a piss-poor mood. But man, she wasn't helping. He didn't need hovering right now. "I'm good," he answered as levelly as he could. Maybe she'd take the hint he wasn't in the mood for friendly. Reaching into the fridge, he pulled out a can of iced tea and a package of ham.

"Sandwich. Here." Her hands covered his. "Let me get it for you. You sit down, and I'll take care of it."

Alex blinked, then slowly counted to ten. He didn't let go of the package, though. He wasn't a kid, and he didn't need to be waited on. He could make his own damned sandwich. Dropping whatever she'd been doing to see to him only made him more annoyed.

Reagan gently tugged on the ham. "I've got it, Alex. What else would you like? I have some potato salad in there, some fruit I can cut up."

For heaven's sake! He grabbed her gently by both shoulders, lifted her a couple inches off the ground, and set her aside, out of his way. "Would you knock it off? I can do for myself. I don't need you to wait on me."

As his voice sharpened with the frustration he tried to hold in check, Reagan's face washed ghost white. He froze, his heart pitching down to his toes. Shit, now he'd hurt her. He shook his head and opened his mouth to apologize.

Before he could get a word out, she backed up a step, a frown pulling at her brow. "Excuse me," she murmured. "I'll just...get out of your way." She pivoted and strode stiffly through the entryway.

Seconds later, he heard her footsteps on the stairs.

"Fuck," he muttered as he set the ham on the counter. *Way to go, asshole.* He'd taken it out on her. Worse, in that split second where her face lost all color, once more he'd witnessed fear shimmering in her eyes.

• • •

Under the cool spray of a shower, Reagan closed her eyes and mentally kicked herself. She'd lost it again. In her defense, she'd never really been around an angry man since Drew's death. She was programmed to default into self-defense mode, and with Drew, if she didn't try to soothe the mood, Lord only knew where it might lead. Guaranteed, it would hurt.

She blew out a hard breath, sending the water that rained down her face scattering. Everything inside her felt shaky. Out of sync. And she was so sick and tired of the reactions she couldn't control. Sick and tired of hiding and lying and evading. Sick and tired of trying to be *normal*. When she wasn't. When she wouldn't ever again be the innocent nineteen-year-old girl who had no idea how harsh the world could be.

She spun off the faucets forcefully, yanked the towel off the door, and then whipped it around her body. Damn Drew. Damn him for dying. Damn him for joining the marines in the first place. Damn him for failing her all the way around and leaving her nothing but broken when she finally had an opportunity for the happiness she fucking deserved.

And yes, she deserved it. She'd forgotten that fact for a while, but relearned it through counseling. She deserved Alex. The way he made her feel. The happiness he brought to her heart.

Biting back a foul oath, she jerked a brush through her hair, fingered a few daubs of gel through the lengths, and sat down on the toilet, frowning as she considered how to undo the error she'd just made in the kitchen. God, what Alex must think. She didn't want to face him after that little display. *Let me get it for you. What do you need?* Reagan wrinkled her nose in distaste. Talk about the epitome of hovering—she'd made a complete fool out of herself.

The only saving grace was that the damned repairman hadn't witnessed her little meltdown. Damage control was limited to Alex. And maybe, just maybe, his bad mood would overpower the incident.

It was time to tell him. Come hell or high water, she couldn't take this any more. Covering her tracks was beginning to snowball. Sooner or later, some excuse would negate another and she'd get caught.

Tonight. When he'd calmed down. She'd tell him tonight.

Meanwhile, she'd keep her distance until he chilled out. If for no other reason than to keep her nerves under control so she didn't do something stupid before then.

Standing, she shoved open the bathroom door and marched to her bedroom. There, she pulled open the closet, and annoyance flared all over again. Every article of clothing she owned was more evidence of the many ways she tried to hide what she'd been through simply so people wouldn't ask. The plain T-shirts, the dresses that covered everything on her backside, the long-sleeved turtlenecks for winter. She jerked one shirt off a hanger and tossed it onto the floor. Then another. And another. She should have cleared them all out months ago, while she was getting rid of the rest of the reminders. Then there wouldn't be room for her to hide from Alex, and she wouldn't be in this predicament.

"Son of a bitch," she muttered as she flung another shirt onto the floor. Who cared if no one believed her? It didn't matter what other people thought—she knew the truth. That was all she needed, and she was done, *done* covering up for Drew Sanders.

Fucking done.

She reached into the shelves along the back wall and pulled out a blue halter top that hadn't seen the light of day in years. It was a cute little thing—ties around the low-cut neck, pretty sparkles that accented the swell of her breasts, and a deep, bare back.

Definitely time to stop hiding. Somewhere along the way, she'd allowed protecting Alex to override protecting herself. She couldn't, *wouldn't,* live that way any longer.

Chapter Seventeen

Footsteps overhead told Alex that Reagan had retreated to her room. Forty-five minutes after blowing up at her, he felt like an ass. It wasn't her fault. She'd just been in the wrong place at the wrong time. Normal couple crossings; everyone went through this once in a while. But he sure as hell felt like shit.

He pushed himself out of the living room chair and headed toward the stairs. From the way she thumped and bumped around, he had a pretty good idea she was pissed off. Not that he blamed her. But he still needed to relay the news about the air-conditioner, and that he'd picked out a new one for her—a decision she'd object to. Before this blew up into a full-scale battle, he intended to cut it off at the pass. Confess his sins, as it were, as opposed to sitting and brooding, waiting for her to come down, her temper worked up in full measure.

With his luck, she wouldn't come down when he finished

confessing, and the trip tomorrow to the party would be full of tension, instead of the relaxing, fun day at the lake it was supposed to be.

Idiot. He muttered beneath his breath as he mounted the stairs.

Still mentally kicking himself, he made his way to Reagan's room and nudged the partially ajar door. It swung inward on a room that appeared empty at first glance.

Muffled cursing deeper within, however, drew him inside. The walk-in closet door stood wide open. Gloriously nude, Reagan stood in the middle, fiddling with something in her hands he couldn't see. His gaze latched onto the sloping curves of her breasts, and his mouth went dry as his cock twitched behind the fly of his jeans. He swallowed hard. *Apologize. Can't touch until you do.*

But damn, it was nice to look. She always kept herself so covered.

She looked up with a squeak, dropped what she held, and jerked a T-shirt over her head. "Alex," she said tensely.

Disappointment swept through him. Her modesty was sweet, in a way, but it drove him nuts. He knew so much about her body, yet she still locked herself away in daylight. *Like she locks everything else away.*

He leaned on the doorframe and folded his arms over his chest. "I'm sorry I snapped at you."

She nodded and bent to pick up the top she'd dropped. The ties dangled from her hands as she folded it, and he found himself wishing she would have put that on, not the plain, uninspiring T-shirt. Then again, this was Reagan, and he couldn't recall ever seeing her in anything that showed any significant amount of skin. The perfect elementary school teacher. He chuckled silently.

"The roof was giving me fits."

Once more, she nodded, but the frown didn't leave her brow. Was she that pissed off? Not good, considering he knew what he had to say next wouldn't go over well at all.

"So…" he began hesitantly. "You need a whole new heating and cooling unit."

Her eyes went wide. "You've got to be kidding me."

"'Fraid not."

She flung the shirt onto the ground. "Damn it!"

He pushed off the doorframe, crossed to her, and wrapped his arms around her. "Easy. It will be all right."

She pushed at his chest. "No, you don't understand. It won't be. I can't afford thousands of dollars of repairs."

Resisting her efforts to break free, Alex held her more securely. They needed to cover this ground, get to the reasons why she couldn't afford the repairs. But though it would piss her off, he could alleviate her worries to some degree. "I took care of it, sweetheart. Ron's bringing a top-of-the-line, energy-efficient unit out this evening if he can get a hold of it."

Reagan shoved hard against him, slipping out of his hold. "You did *what*?"

He blinked. He'd expected annoyance, but not the angry heat flaring in her gaze. "I took care of it. You were asleep."

"It's *my* air-conditioner."

Really? "It's a damned air-conditioner. Not a couch you look at every day. Not carpeting. Not goddamned wallpaper or the style of your front porch. Did you want me to send him away and let it wait another day? You were *sleeping*."

"You could have woken me!"

"What the hell is the big deal?" Exasperation hit him like an iron fist to the gut. For Christ's sake, he was trying to help her out. "You ignore the rest of everything around you—the roof, the porch, the tree, not to mention Drew's death, but you're going to take notice of this? What the hell?"

She threw her hands up in the air. "It's the principle—this is *my* house. I appreciate your help, but you can't come in here and just take over."

"It's *my* money. If I want to buy you the best system for the cost, that's my choice, not yours."

She shook her head and stormed past him. "No, it's not. I have a say. And if I want the worst system available, but the cheapest one, then that's what goes into my house."

He followed on her heels as she stalked down the stairs. "That's absurd."

"Maybe. But it's my decision."

As she reached the bottom stair, he caught her wrist and turned her around hastily. She recoiled and jerked free. Alex stared, searching her face for answers. What in the world had gotten into her? It was a box. A simple machine. Why in the hell was she acting like he'd stripped all her control out of her hands?

• • •

Reagan checked herself, stopping the instinctual reaction to duck as her shoulders tensed. She would *not* cower. No more than she would allow a man to run her life. Alex might not understand because he lacked the greater perspective, but now, in the heat of this argument, wasn't the time to drop that bomb on him. She stood still, her body as unyielding as her position. "I need to run my own life."

His mouth pursed as he closed his eyes. Then, whatever he tried to bite back exploded free. "Then do so!"

"What?" she cried. "I *am*."

"No, you're not." He strode across the living room to the bare place on the wall where Drew's flag had hung. "Where is the flag, Reagan? Where is *Drew*? You're avoiding everything. Ignoring it like the box of clothes you packed away."

She stared, speechless. That's what he thought? That she couldn't acknowledge Drew's death? She shook off her shock. "He's dead. In the ground. I'm moving *forward.*" Damned if that didn't sound cold, but there was no way around the truth of it. "You're the one who can't let go. You cling to his memory like you can wish him back."

"If I could, I *would.* He saved my life! But you wouldn't wish him back, would you?"

Pain sliced at her. If Drew were here, Alex and she would have never discovered what they had between them. Did he really regret their involvement so much?

She couldn't answer his question, not without destroying him, as well as what he thought of her, completely. Instead, she bit down on her lower lip and turned for the kitchen. "I can't wish him back, Alex. Neither can you."

"Fuck!" His oath echoed from the other room, followed by a muffled *thump*. Had he just hit something?

Illogical fear raced down her spine. Had he wanted to hit *her*? Like Drew, had he been stripped of his decency in the marines? He'd assumed she wanted the best air-conditioner available. On the surface, it was a small thing. But he'd taken the control out of her hands, made decisions for her, and that was no little detail. Maybe he was more like Drew than she'd recognized. After all, birds of a feather…

Footsteps announced his presence in the doorway. She yanked open the fridge for a beer, jerked the cap off, and chugged down a deep gulp.

"Reagan," he said more calmly. "This is crazy. We don't need to fight about this."

She shook her head. "I don't care if it sounds crazy, if *I* sound crazy. It matters to me. Don't you *dare* come here and try to take control of my life. Despite how you see it, that's what you did."

He spluttered something nonsensical and clenched a hand at his thigh. Reagan's eyes locked on that tight fist. Her stomach quivered. *He won't hit you. He's not Drew. And if he does, you can send him to jail. You don't have to defend him.* She inhaled deeply, set her beer on the counter. Before she completely lost it, she needed space.

She stalked to the back door. "I'm going to Desi's. We both need to cool off."

Not giving him time to protest, she stormed out the door and pulled it shut behind her. Maybe she did sound a bit insane—to someone who hadn't suffered what she had, who didn't even know, she likely would. All the more reason to tell him the truth. She could deal with Shelley thinking she was crazy—Shelley wasn't part of her life anymore. But not Alex. Alex meant too much. And right now, she was too wound up to delve into that conversation. Once she'd gathered her thoughts, once she'd chased back the irrational fear skittering through her veins, they'd talk.

She'd tell him everything he never wished to know.

Chapter Eighteen

Reagan slid her back porch door open at ten minutes after ten. Her house was quiet, the lights in the front room dim. A mechanical hum filled the silence, and the air held a chill that hadn't been present in several weeks. Alex had gone ahead with the install. She breathed deeply, accepting that fact. Hours of conversation with Desi, along with several tears, made her accept that she'd overreacted. Unlike Drew, Alex acted out of the kindness of his heart.

She'd just been too stunned to realize it earlier. Too unprepared for his generosity. And she'd made a complete fool out of herself.

Time to confess her shame. The wine flowing through her veins offered courage, yet even it didn't erase the nervous tremble in her legs that intensified with each step closer to home. Her hand shook as she turned around to close the door behind her.

She took a steady step toward the living room, half

hoping Alex wouldn't be there.

When she entered and found the couch empty, no sign of his meager things, her heart stopped. She squeezed her eyes shut, blocking out the signs of abandonment.

So he'd left.

Regret stormed through her, and her shoulders bowed with the weight of it. She supposed she shouldn't have expected him to stay, not after the way she'd reacted to something so benign. She'd even prepared herself for him to walk out the door once he knew the secrets she harbored.

But she hadn't anticipated the emptiness that would come with his leaving. The absolute, utter, bereft feeling. Life had changed in the few days he occupied her world. For the better. She believed in happiness again, *tasted* it.

She'd never imagined his absence could be so...tangible.

On legs that felt leaden, she crossed to the front door to lock it and pull down the shade. She turned off the solitary lamp on the table, the *click* ringing out ominously. Like a tumbler on the lock to her life. Encapsulating her in solitude.

Well. She'd asked for it. She had no one to blame but herself. Desi would tell her that in the morning.

She climbed the stairs to the bedroom, her steps dogged. Her bed would be just as empty. Barren. She gave herself a mental kick as tears threatened. She would not cry. They were better off this way. Alex could go on, his faith in Drew untainted. She could move forward, find someone who couldn't be chased away by a ghost.

But that someone would never be Alex.

Reagan pushed open the door to her bedroom, her vision fuzzy. She blinked back the rising tears and slipped inside, thankful the darkness cloaked the place where she and

Alex had made love so passionately. She didn't want to see the empty pillow beside hers.

She pushed the door closed heavily.

Her sheets rustled. Alex's gravelly voice rasped, "Reagan?"

She whirled to face the bed. *Oh, God.* Her heart jumped to her throat as tears coursed down her cheeks. She rushed to the bed and threw herself on it.

Alex caught her against his chest. His strong arms held her tight. All the anger she'd felt earlier, the loss of control, the fear, dissolved into meaningless nothing as his warmth enveloped her.

"I thought you'd left," she choked out, her nose buried against the side of his neck.

He smoothed a hand down her hair. "I don't walk out on arguments," he murmured, his voice clogged with sleep. "I hope you don't mind I abandoned the couch."

She shook her head, too consumed with emotion to find words, and clung to him more tightly.

As if sensing the depth of feeling coursing through her, he wrapped her more securely into his arms. They lay that way for several long moments, as Reagan struggled to pull herself together.

"I'm sorry," she muttered through her tears. "I overreacted."

"Shh." His fingers combed through her hair. "We've both had a taxing day. We'll talk about it in the morning."

"But I—"

Alex shifted position as he set his fingers beneath her chin and tipped her face to his. In the next instant, his mouth dusted across hers. "In the morning, sweetheart." His mouth clasped hers again, the tug of his teeth begging for entrance.

She yielded to his silent request and couldn't hold in a quiet mewl of pleasure as his tongue tangled with hers. His fingers threaded through her hair, holding her in place, his grip firm but not painful. Slowly, languorously, he possessed her, filling her veins with insatiable craving. She'd thought she'd lost him. Had come so close to creating her own misery.

Slow and sweet gave way to a hungrier demand, and urgency laced his kiss. Could he, too, have shared the same fear?

With a low groan, he dragged her atop his body so she straddled his hips. His fingers kneaded her bottom, the same hint of threadbare control in their tight clasp and release. Need swept her into a riptide of yearning, and Reagan tipped forward, stroking herself against the hard length of his cock. Alex's body twitched beneath her.

He tore his mouth away, his breath rasping like sandpaper. In the light of the moon, she glimpsed the dark intensity of his gaze. The heat there, the undeniable passion, made her shiver.

He said nothing as he lifted one hand and cupped her breast through her raggedy T-shirt. The silence added another layer of intimacy that frayed her nerve endings. When he swept a thumb over her hardened nipple, blissful shock coursed through her body. She gasped, then shuddered. "Alex," she whispered raggedly.

He dropped his hands to the waistband of her shorts and fumbled at the button with shaking fingers. With a frustrated grunt, he dropped his hands. "Help," he muttered.

Any other time, she might have laughed. But the desperation beneath his hoarse request somehow made him more…human. And the evidence of his powerful desire only made hers burn hotter. She hurriedly complied, shimmying out of the shorts and tossing them onto the floor.

When she climbed over him again, bare skin brushed the inside of her thighs. He'd cast off his boxers, and his hard cock nestled against her sex. The warmth of that rigid length, the promised pleasure his body offered, was a temptation she couldn't ignore. Driven by sheer instinct, she slid along his length, drawing from him a throaty groan.

His hands latched onto her hips. He tipped upward, stroking her clit in return, and provoking her into a needy whimper. As she sank against his body, aching for the full-on contact, he denied her. He lifted her up, and in one smooth stroke, impaled her.

Reagan cried out in ecstasy.

"God, you feel so damned good," he ground out through clenched teeth. His fingers held her tight, pressing against her hip bones, rocking her in time to the motion of his body and his deep, possessive thrusts.

Makeup sex. She'd never known this sort of bliss. But it engulfed her like a wave crashing on a rocky shore. She braced her hands on his shoulders and closed her eyes on another uncontrollable shudder. Levering herself with her bent knees, she countered his strokes, letting sensation consume her. Quiet sounds of pleasure rumbled in the back of Alex's throat. His teeth sank into his lower lip, and his jaw tensed. Evidence of his faltering control.

When she slid down him again and twisted her hips, he hissed. Beneath her bottom, his thighs trembled.

"Fuck," he exhaled. "Reagan, I…"

With another hoarse oath, he crushed her to his body and flipped her onto her back. She wound her arms around his neck, curling her nails into his nape and wrapping her ankles around his waist. Their mouths crashed together as his body drove into hers recklessly. She met him thrust for thrust, racing toward a cataclysmic end. The tremor in his arms told her he fought the same futile battle against release.

She didn't want him to fight it, though. She wanted him undone, completely exposed, raw and aching like she was, and she bucked beneath him, pushing him into a frenetic pace. He slammed into her, jostling the bed. Again. And again. She cried out each time he hit her most sensitive spot, pleasure saturating her awareness.

Once more he slammed home, and Reagan splintered apart with a sharp cry. Distantly, she heard his guttural shout. Felt the way his body stiffened like stone.

And then she was tumbling down from the high precipice of rapture, sliding her hands down Alex's sweat-slickened spine, and landing safely, tenderly, in his warm embrace. His mouth caught hers, softer, gentler. Sweeter. Their tongues danced slowly as her heart stumbled into a steadier beat. He stretched out alongside her, carrying her with him, and wrapped her in the protective cocoon of his strong arms. Then, he broke the kiss, releasing her lips as if he despised the thought of separation.

"You are amazing," he whispered, rubbing his cheek against hers.

Through her exhaustion, Reagan smiled. "So are you, Alex," she murmured. "So are you."

He grunted, but offered no other objection. She forced her eyes to stay open, despite the gut-deep longing to let her lashes fall and give over to sleep. After a few silent moments, his breathing leveled off, and the weight of his arm increased. It required every ounce of willpower she pos-sessed to duck from beneath his hold and slip out of the bed. But she didn't dare tempt fate by sleeping in just the shirt. She slid back into her shorts, tucked the backside of the shirttail in the waistband, and then, finally, crawled back into his heavenly embrace.

Chapter Nineteen

When the air-conditioner hummed to life at nine the next morning, Reagan sat up in bed and pushed her hair out of her face. The birds were in full melody, and the sun shone bright. Alex wasn't beside her, but his side of the bed was still warm. She guessed he was outside, assessing what else he could do with her porch. Strangely, she no longer felt threatened by his involvement. Somewhere in the night, tangled around his warm, hard body, she made peace with it.

Today was his birthday party, and she was determined to make the best of it. They needed to talk, to have a good long heart-to-heart, and she was ready now. But she'd let him make that move, bring the subject up, since he'd been so adamant to put it to bed last night. Given her irrational behavior last night, she wouldn't be surprised if he decided not to take her along today.

Her stomach rumbled, reminding her all she'd had for dinner the night before was too many glasses of wine.

She'd been dying to try a homemade cinnamon roll recipe for months. Now that the air-conditioning was working, she didn't have to worry about heating up the house with the oven. Or standing over a hot stove, sweating.

And maybe, just maybe, she could kick off the day doing something nice for Alex. He'd been so considerate, and she so reactive—he deserved a little special treatment.

Reagan took a deep breath, climbed out of bed, and opened her bedroom door, still dressed in the clothes she'd worn the day before. Wrinkled, rumpled, and likely her hair was a nest of tangles. But her stomach wouldn't wait for a shower.

The hallway was cold enough she shivered. She'd definitely have to adjust the thermostat—what had Ron and Alex left it on, fifty?

No, sixty-eight, she discovered as she stopped at the bottom of the stairs. She moved it up to seventy-three, then stole a glance around the living room. A shadow moved outside her window. *Alex.* She smiled to herself, continued on to the kitchen, and fished the recipe out of a three-ring binder. The one good thing she could say about Drew—when he did come home, he always managed to create a reason for her to do the one hobby she loved most.

She placed the book on the counter and paused, her gaze fixed on the doorway. Nerves spiked. What if he was still upset? What if he wanted to talk right now?

No, she wouldn't get wound up. She was going to be normal. At whatever cost. Which meant cinnamon rolls. And after that, her sapling in the front yard could probably use a decent watering. If not it, then the flowers.

Normal. You can do this. You know how.

• • •

Alex finally wrested the last dangerous board free and tossed it aside. He opened the front door and hesitated, a smile pulling at his mouth. The sound of Reagan puttering around in the kitchen, banging pans, clattering bowls, running the sink faucet, was growing on him. That little racket of mundane routine brought a certain peace to the topsy-turvy emotions roiling through him.

Yesterday had been a doozy. Last night, her tears unwound something balled up tight inside him. He never wanted to hear her cry again. And whatever prompted that stupid argument yesterday—he'd never allow that to happen again, either.

For whatever reason, Reagan felt oppressed. If she needed wings, then by God, he'd give them to her. Today would be a start, once he brought Shelley back into contact with her.

A sudden realization made him blink. He'd first met Reagan at the lake where Diane planned the party. What a fitting place for beginnings. Maybe she'd recognize that, too, though he didn't intend to come off as a sap by pointing it out.

The nagging voice of reason reminded him Drew's death might turn her away from him, forever. He shoved it aside. He'd broach that later. When it was absolutely necessary. Right now, whatever she was cooking was a siren's song to his stomach. It rumbled loudly as the aroma filled his nose. *Cinnamon.*

He eased through the entryway to the kitchen, investigating the enticing scent. She stood at the counter, flour dotting her cheeks, still dressed in the comfortable clothes from the day before.

"That smells delicious," he murmured, stepping deeper into the room.

She stopped, cocked her head, and gave him a grin. "We'll find out together. I've never made them before. Happy birthday, by the way."

He chuckled as he lowered himself onto a seat at the high counter. "Thanks. We'll have to leave in about an hour. If that's not enough time, we can be late."

She shook her head. "No, that's fine. Can you watch these while I hit the shower?"

"Only if you kiss me." He caught a flour-covered hand and guided her around the corner of the bar.

Pressing her other flour-splattered hand to his chest, she grinned and then kissed him swiftly and soundly. "How's that?"

Alex grunted. He glanced down where her hand pressed into his pectoral and gave her a false look of annoyance. "Unlike you, I don't like to wear my food." He plucked her hand off his body, lifted it to his lips, and drew her index finger into his mouth. Holding her gaze, he swirled his tongue around the elegant digit before slowly sliding it out. "I prefer to eat it."

Reagan giggled and nudged her way between his parted knees. He secured his hands on the slope of her hips. With one dip of his head, he captured her mouth and drew her into a slow, sensual kiss that threatened to eradicate his senses. His heart kicked hard. Heat flooded his veins. God, he was so damn hungry for her.

As his hands moved of their own volition, sliding to the

toned muscling of her ass, he forced himself to draw away. They had tonight to indulge—a full, uninterrupted night he intended to make full use of. At the moment, more important things needed to be said.

Alex held her smoldering gaze. "I'm sorry about yesterday."

She tensed in his hands.

He rushed on before she could respond. "You're right—I knew you'd be annoyed, and I went ahead anyway. I don't think I really understood how important it was to you. I won't do it again."

Reagan leaned in and relaxed against him. "I'm sorry, too. I overreacted. Drew…was so adamant…so stubborn." She spoke slowly, as if every word required intense consideration. "I've gotten used to…making my own decisions."

He tugged her in close and kissed her softly. "Honest miscommunication. Let's not dwell on it."

Nodding, she backed out of his embrace. "I'll go change."

He tipped his head, studying her, knowing she'd choose another loose, comfortable T-shirt and a pair of irresistible shorts. The shorts he liked—a lot. But she had such a gorgeous body it was a shame she didn't show it off a little. "I really liked that halter top you had in your closet yesterday."

"That thing?" Her eyes widened as she let out a tight laugh. "It's so old."

"It's cute."

With the same speculative tip of her head, she regarded him thoughtfully. "I guess I could take a sweater if it gets cold."

"You could." He offered nothing more. To do so approached dangerous waters. He didn't want her thinking he was some sort of control freak who wanted to dictate what she wore and when. It would just be nice to see her not hiding in shapeless shirts for a little bit.

After another stretched-out moment, she nodded and turned for the stairs. "I'll see what I can come up with."

Alex blinked, scarcely able to believe she'd agreed to consider it. To Reagan, that amount of skin must be scandalous. Yet she had. And he had the distinct impression she'd done it *for him.* Emotion tightened his chest. Such a simple thing. Profoundly meaningful all the same. He couldn't remember when anyone had done anything just for him before this week with Reagan.

Rising from the high-top stool, he gave in to a smile. Today, he could return that same feeling of appreciation. Diane phoned last night; she'd reached Shelley. After further talking with Jacob, Diane had managed to throw together more or less what amounted to a commemoration for Drew. Nothing formal, just a gathering of friends who'd cared for him. It would do Reagan good to have an opportunity to reconnect with everyone. To see beyond the loss she'd experienced and perhaps stop hiding from reality. Grieving meant living— only it had taken him until last night to realize that truth.

Now, to get her there and show her just how willing he was to move forward with her. To embrace all the hurdles, all the insecurities, to even risk confessing his ultimate failure with Drew—he didn't want to keep it secret any longer. To have a chance at this, whatever it was, she deserved the same open honesty he demanded of her. It would tear him to pieces, but at least she'd know the man he was, not the hero she envisioned. If she didn't want him after, well, he'd cope with the pain. Somehow.

Chapter Twenty

As Alex's pickup rolled to an easy stop before a grassy picnic area in Chain O'Lakes State Park, Reagan took in the lush surroundings with a soft smile. She'd met Alex the first time here. He'd invited Drew and her up on a weekend during leave. In water, splashing and dunking with the guys, she'd been captivated by Alex. His easy laughter, his friendly warmth, held charm she couldn't ignore. The troubles had only started in her marriage, the abuse just beginning. A shove here and there. Unjustified actions. One open hand across her face. That night…things changed. Her behavior earned her the first meeting with Drew's belt. This place held memories. Both those she longed to forget, and those she never wanted to let go.

At the conflicting thought, she drew in an uneasy breath and tugged her navy blue cardigan around her shoulders more securely. She'd given in to wearing the damn halter top, but now she second-guessed that decision. Though her back remained covered, she felt exposed.

She closed her eyes, mentally reciting all the reasons she'd let herself be lured out of her protective shell. Alex had proven he wasn't Drew. He'd apologized. He wasn't the kind of guy who'd make decisions for her, wouldn't ever try to control her or assume what she needed. She'd worn the damn top as a means of showing she really forgave him, but that didn't mean she had to take the sweater off.

His hand brushed her thigh, just beneath the hem of her short denim shorts. "You'll like Diane, Luke, and Mom."

From the stories about his childhood and his polar-opposite brother, she had no doubt she would. She honestly couldn't wait to meet his brother. His sister's insatiable curiosity, though, stretched her nerves. Reagan only hoped Diane wouldn't start asking questions about why she'd worn a sweater when the temperature pushed ninety.

She forced a smile, hoping it didn't come across strained. "Lead the way." Beyond the tall grasses of the picnic shelter, the lake glistened invitingly.

He let himself out and came around to her side before she could open the door all the way. He propped it open with one hand, extending the other for hers. Reagan slipped her fingers into his palm, and a sense of confidence, of *rightness* stole over her. Trepidation vanished as she stepped onto the gravel parking lot. She was with *Alex*, where she'd always longed to be. Meeting his family—people whom she felt she already knew after all the tales he'd told through the years. Last night, they'd tackled a hurdle and overcome it. She was ready for this.

She wanted to be here more than anything.

Clasping his hand more securely, she gave him a genuine

grin and rose on tiptoe to brush a kiss across his mouth. He didn't hesitate to welcome her advance. Curving his hand around the small of her back, he bent her closer, tugged her lower lip between his teeth, and drew her into a tantalizing kiss. A kiss that proved to her he'd somehow come to terms with the ghost of their shared past. And proved it to his family.

When he released her mouth, he held her close a moment longer. His gaze held hers, conveying words she couldn't quite decipher, but she understood the broader meaning. Affection glinted there. No, more than affection. Something…deeper.

"Let's eat," he whispered as he stepped back and away.

Still holding fast to her hand, he led her around the front of the pickup and to a shelter tucked beneath tall shade trees. Children's laughter echoed on the gentle breeze. At least three dozen people milled around the wooden tables, paper plates of food already in hand.

Reagan identified Diane instantly—her spiky platinum hair gave her away. Alex had made it sound over-the-top, but the style held class and taste. The way she rushed toward her brother, a grin stretching from ear to ear, hinted at her friendliness.

"Reagan," she cried, arms outstretched. "Oh my God, it's so nice to finally meet you. I've heard so many stories over the years. Of you. Of Drew." Diane dragged her into a fierce hug. "I'm so sorry for what you've been through."

Sorry? Reagan fumbled for a response. Had Diane not seen the way she'd just been kissing Alex? There was nothing to be remotely sorry for.

She finally found her tongue, and as she backed out of

the hug managed a polite, "Thank you." Maybe she'd been too far away to observe the kiss.

The way Diane met Alex's gaze and her smile turned smug, however, suggested she knew every detail. Reagan's nerves twisted her belly into knots all over again. Would his family think it was too soon? Would they question whether Alex and she had ever been more than friends?

"Alex!"

She pushed the worries aside as another voice carried to where they stood. A voice she recognized.

She swung around to find Jacob standing beneath the edge of the shelter roof, waving Alex down. What was he doing here?

Diane kissed Alex's cheek. "Happy birthday, little man."

He returned her gesture of sibling affection with a one-armed hug. "Thanks." He paused, then added, "For everything."

Jacob hustled over, clasped Alex's hand, and pumped it enthusiastically. "Man, what an awesome idea. No one hardly spoke at the funeral. Everyone's telling stories, laughing — it's what Drew would have wanted."

Drew. Funeral. A chill stole down Reagan's spine. She looked beyond Alex to the people gathered under and around the shelter. Don from the hardware store. A handful of other vets sitting in the far corner. Other faces she recognized — friends of Drew's. Chance. Desi.

As her gaze fell on her friend, Desi shoved off a bench seat and rushed across the short distance of grass. Spots of crimson flushed her cheeks, and her eyes flashed with anger. She wedged herself between Reagan and Alex and gave him a scathing glare. Then she turned to Reagan, and her expression twisted with concern. "Are you okay? I only heard about it this morning. I called to warn you, but your cell phone's off."

Behind her, Chance approached at a more cautious speed, his gaze narrowed and assessing. The tight downturn of his mouth hinted at tightly controlled anger.

"What's going on, Desi?" Reagan asked, looking over her shoulder at Alex, asking him more than her. Instinct told her she already knew.

His grin slipped. A tight frown pursed his lips.

Desi spun on him, her voice sharp and incredulous. "You didn't warn her? Can you be any more insensitive?"

"Warn me about what?"

"Damn it," Desi muttered before she set both hands on Reagan's shoulders and regret washed across her face. "This isn't a birthday party, sweetie. Alex and his sister put together a commemoration for Drew." Once more, she glared at Alex, then at Diane. "Evidently without telling you. Half of Colton is here, and so is—"

Shelley.

Reagan's gaze locked on a lithe brunette standing at the edge of the refreshment table. She held a plastic cup in her hand and stared, expression full of loathing, at where Reagan and Alex stood. Reagan didn't need anyone to tell her—Shelley had most definitely witnessed that kiss.

The ground beneath Reagan's feet felt unsteady as the deeper meaning of Desi's explanation sank home. Alex had coordinated this. For almost a full week, she'd done everything she could to drive the point home she didn't care to discuss Drew. Yet he'd gone behind her back and planned this little event, dragging her along as if he presumed she'd be elated.

Unable to believe what she was hearing, Reagan turned imploring eyes on him. "Tell me she's not right. Tell me you didn't do this."

Diane rushed to answer, even as Alex's expression tightened. "You've been dealing with so much, Reagan, Alex thought you'd enjoy the chance to reconnect with friends. He said you were so sad that you'd lost touch with Shelley, and he asked me to invite her to his birthday party. After talking to her and Jacob, everything took a different angle."

So, Alex had his sister contact Shelley. In the back of her mind, Reagan knew she shouldn't be angry with him—he had no way of knowing what Drew's sister had put her through. That she'd be more than content to never see the woman again. But no amount of logic could override the deep-rooted fury, the utter sense of betrayal that swirled in her gut. She twisted her hand free from his and stalked away.

To go where? She couldn't run. She couldn't hide in his pickup. His entire family was here, along with too many other people. Four steps from where she'd been standing, she stopped.

Desi and Chance appeared at her side. Her hand slipped around Reagan's elbow, and she slowly turned Reagan to face her. Chance rested a heavy, encouraging hand on Reagan's opposite shoulder.

"I found out literally right before we left," Desi said. "Diane called Chance this morning while I was at the store. He didn't know what to do, so he said we'd come."

"We weren't conspiring against you," Chance added with a squeeze of his fingers. "We're in your corner, kid."

Reagan inhaled long and slow. Lifting her shoulders, she

steeled her spine and sighed. "I know."

"If you want to go home, we'll take you." Desi's rich brown eyes filled with sympathy. "But I know you can make it through this, if you want to stay."

"I know that, too," Reagan murmured.

Why had Alex done this? Her gaze tracked back to him, and she took in the hurt that pulled at the corners of his eyes. He thought he'd done something to make her happy—and that was the crux of it all. Once again, he'd made decisions on her behalf, acted as if he knew what was best for her. Even after this morning, when he'd promised not to do so again.

Alex was more like Drew than Reagan cared to admit. And she should have seen it all along.

"I'm not running away." With a disparaging shake of her head, she stalked toward the refreshment table, hoping someone had at least thought to bring beer. But instead, all she found was iced tea, soda of all different flavors, and water. She yanked a cup off the stack and filled it with grape soda, then chugged it like a bottle of pale ale. She'd smile and say all the appropriate things people expected—she would *not* hide. But when it was over, when Alex had taken her back home, there would be no misunderstandings between them. She'd tell him Drew's true character, right as she told him to get the hell out.

For now, she had a role to play. One she knew all too well. A few more hours of keeping Drew's secrets, because some small part of her respected the soldier. Then she would finally be free.

Chapter Twenty-One

"She's something, Alex. Strong. Easy on the eyes. What's she see in you?"

The sound of his brother's voice rumbling near his shoulder startled Alex. He turned to face Luke, struggling to hide the fact that he'd been staring off where Reagan sat near the lake with his sister's twin girls and her son. With a forced chuckle, he gave his older brother a noncommittal shrug. "She knows a good thing when she sees it."

Luke's mouth twisted with a smirk. "Smart-ass."

Yeah, he was. At the moment, though, he needed the confidence that came with brotherly banter. Something was off with her. Sure, she smiled and carried on polite conversation, acted every bit as friendly as he remembered her. But chilly distance clouded her eyes. She hardly had three words to say to him directly, though she stayed at his side as if she belonged there.

Just like she used to be.

And that was the bitch of it—she was exactly the Reagan he remembered from barbecues with Drew. Not the Reagan he'd discovered this past week at her home. So why the hell did the woman he watched now feel like a stranger?

Because of this party. Because he'd forced her to confront Drew.

Annoyance flickered all over again. Couldn't she see that locking it away wasn't healthy? All the people here today had shed tears—himself included—but they weren't the bitter kind. Reagan, alone, remained dry-eyed. Like she didn't even care.

Hell, she hadn't even spoken to Shelley once.

His gaze pulled back to her in time to see her throw her head back in laughter, and then tackle the eight-year-old Benjamin. He went down squealing and squirming in a fit of uncontrollable giggles. Damn, she was even playing like nothing else occurred around her.

"She's not just Drew's widow, is she?"

Luke assessed Alex with a cool blue stare. When Alex didn't flinch, his brother's gaze narrowed.

Ugh. Alex nearly groaned aloud. He choked the rising sound down before it could escape and huffed a sigh. "It's complicated."

Frowning, he looked back at Reagan. Behind her, the sun rode low on the water, casting bronze color over the grassy area. The sunlight danced off her hair, making it shine like spun gold. Her skin held a warm glow that gave her an ethereal appearance, and there was something so compelling about the way she interacted with his nieces and nephew that Alex's heart swelled painfully. All four sat on the green grass, hands propped behind their backs and staring up at an orange-and-lavender sky, occasionally pointing at big fluffy clouds.

Falsely oblivious. His heart twisted at the picture she presented. A contrast of warmth and coldness. Distance and closeness. How could she pretend so easily?

Or could it be possible she really didn't care?

That thought left a bitter taste in his mouth. She should care. Drew had been her husband. He'd worshipped the ground she walked on. To be so…ambivalent after his death…

"Hey, Alex," a soft, feminine voice called from behind.

Luke stepped back as Shelley approached.

Her soft brown eyes offered sympathy. She set a hand on his arm and maneuvered even closer, silently, yet deliberately, pushing his brother further aside. "How are you doing? I should have called." Shelley blew out a sigh. "It's just…"

"Hard," he finished for her. "I should have called, too. I get it."

Nodding, she folded her arms over her breasts and gazed out at the water, in the general direction where Reagan romped with the kids.

Alex looked after her, heaviness settling on his shoulders. "I don't understand, Shelley. Reagan acts like nothing happened. She doesn't even want to talk about Drew. I thought she'd be happy to see you, and she hasn't even said hello, has she?"

"No, and she won't."

He arched an eyebrow. "That doesn't make sense."

"She's unstable." Turning to face him, she leveled him with a hard frown. "Drew had to lock her out of their finances. She spends like it's water. When he did that, she made up all kinds of terrible things about him."

Shock jammed a fist in Alex's gut. Reagan? Mentally unstable? Drew hadn't been joking all along with his remarks on finances. Her reaction, when Alex handed her his credit card, suddenly made more sense. Along with the weirdness at the ice cream shop. But still—unstable? Making up things about Drew? He squinted at Shelley. "What kind of things?"

• • •

Reagan snagged Benjamin around the waist as he darted past. His laughter rang with hers, lightening the dark cloud around her spirits. All afternoon, she'd heard nothing but praise for Drew, and it required every ounce of willpower she possessed to keep her tongue in check and smile and nod politely. Escape came with the children.

She used Benjamin's imprisoned state to her advantage and tickled his ribs. He squealed and twisted until he hung half sideways in the air. His sisters broke into laughter as he flailed, trying to escape Reagan's deft fingers.

As the twins giggled gleefully and swept in on the fun, Reagan rocked back on her heels. Her gaze locked on Alex, and she bristled. He stood beside Shelley, his brother only a few paces behind. No doubt recounting Drew's successes on the battlefield or his medals again. Her stomach twisted. She couldn't take much more hero worship.

Best not to leave them alone, though. Knowing Alex, he'd ask some question Shelley would be more than happy to twist.

Standing, Reagan dusted the sand off her hands and inclined her head toward their mother. "Kids, why don't you three go on back. I need to talk to your uncle for a bit."

She drew in a deep breath and started toward Alex, doing her best to appear nonchalant. He'd turned once again, as had Shelley, and their backs were to her. His brother listened raptly, his line of sight to Reagan blocked by Alex's broad shoulders.

Reagan stopped five feet away as Shelley's words reached her ears.

"Yes, really. I couldn't believe it. She called *me* with something so preposterous. Drew would never hit a woman."

Reagan's mouth dropped open. Shelley had told Alex? She blinked. In a hundred years, she never would have believed the woman would spill those secrets in public. Or even semipublic.

"That's nuts," Alex muttered. "He saved puppies. He'd no more hit Reagan than he would skin a cat."

"Exactly," Shelley continued, nodding. "He adored her. When I told him, he explained her father was an abuser and she, well, it affected her. She used it as an excuse for pity—to get what she wanted."

Stunned to the depths of her being, Reagan stared wide-eyed. *To get what she wanted.* Oh, fucking hell, no. Judging from the astonishment written all over Alex's face, he was buying into her ridiculous story as well. Fury surged through her veins. She might not have told him Drew's dark habits, but she'd given him no reason to doubt her mental stability. Yet there he stood, shaking his head in that flabbergasted way that said he refused to even entertain the possibility his best friend might have been an abuser.

Damn him. Damn her. She'd had enough of being targeted. Of being discounted. She'd suffered Shelley's humiliation once before. She would not do so again. Drew's secrets weren't sacred. Not anymore. She stalked forward, driven by sheer rage.

"Is that so, Shelley?" she called out, scathingly. "I made it up?"

"Reagan," Alex said slowly.

She whirled on him. "Don't you *dare* Reagan me. You want the damned truth? I'll show you the truth!" Before she fully realized what she was doing, she jerked her sweater off, threw it on the ground, and presented her back.

Chapter Twenty-Two

Alex stared, temporarily robbed of thought by the silvery-gray scars covering Reagan's back. Tiny horseshoe-shaped imprints marred her fair skin from her shoulder blades to the base of her spine. A faint few still held a pinkish hue. It almost looked like she'd fallen off a motorcycle and ended up with a bad case of road rash. Almost. But those little horseshoe shapes looked more familiar. Something he recognized but couldn't place. Definitely not rocks, though.

"What is that?" he blurted as Shelley let out a strangled gasp.

She spun to face him and rasped, "It's ugly, isn't it?"

He tensed, his stomach twisting. Why, he wasn't quite certain. But it was like that bad feeling beyond the wire all over again. Something was coming. Aimed directly for him. "I don't...understand."

"Reagan, this isn't the place—" Shelley warned tightly. "Don't start this here."

"Isn't the place?" Bending, Reagan swiped her sweater off the ground and balled it in her hands. "When is the place to tell you what your venerated brother did to me? Look close. It's a fucking belt, Shelley. It was Drew's favorite way to punish me." She glared at Alex. "And now you know why I don't give a damn he's gone. Why I never want to talk about him. I'm not *avoiding* his death. I'm celebrating my freedom!"

Oh, holy fuck no. His world pitched sideways. He blinked, then blinked again, trying to swallow the undeniable proof someone had beaten her. Shelley claimed it was her father. But he'd never known Reagan to lie.

"No," he whispered.

"Yes," she ground out tightly. "There are a few marks here for looking at you too long. And at Santa at the mall, and the fucking grocery sacker, and take your damn pick." She shouldered around him as she yanked the sweater back on. "I'm going home."

"Jesus," Luke muttered, his voice barely audible.

"It's something else," Shelley proclaimed, stubbornly refusing to acknowledge the evidence. "Drew would never hit a woman. You're crazy, Reagan."

But it wasn't something else. It couldn't be—Reagan did not lie. She avoided. She distracted. She *hid* things.

But she'd lied about Drew's snoring.

Yet those horseshoe brands...Alex's stomach twisted harder. Drew? An abuser? He owed his life to a man who'd beaten his wife? Who'd beaten *Reagan?*

It couldn't be possible. Her father, though...

"Screw you, Shelley," Reagan muttered. Her angry glare locked on Alex again, narrowing even more. "And screw you, too, for even considering I might make something like this up. For standing here and *allowing* her to defame me. Good-bye, Alex."

She stormed off, long legs crossing the tall grass with determined purpose. Alex stared, unable to move. The way she'd flinched on her porch scalded through his memory. Her oddness over being handed a twenty-dollar bill. He couldn't deny it if he wanted to. And yet…he couldn't accept it, either.

Looking at you too long.

Surely, she hadn't said that. He must have imagined it. Drew wouldn't have assumed anything brewed between them.

Then again…

He forced his feet into motion, following after her. "Wait." He caught her by the elbow. "Just wait a damned minute."

She turned, her anger muted by the shimmering of tears within her eyes. "What?" she whispered.

He searched her face but found no answers. "If this is true, why didn't you tell me?"

She shook her head. "What was I supposed to say?" She blew out a hard breath and pushed her hair off her shoulders. "The look on your face now—I didn't want to put that there."

"You *looked* at me too long?" he barked.

Closing her eyes, Reagan nodded. "But it wasn't just you. Drew changed after he enlisted. At least I like to think he changed. Maybe he didn't. Maybe he was always an abuser. But that's the truth of it—he was. He controlled everything I did with that belt. In the end, he cut me off financially, convinced his family I was mentally ill, and left me in this mess you've stumbled into."

"Cut you off financially? Where did his insurance policy and death benefits go—those don't just disappear."

"Drew made Shelley the beneficiary to his life insurance. And his beneficiary in all other things, too." She clenched her teeth, no doubt biting back the anger that turned her voice brittle. "It was another way of controlling me. He wouldn't hand over money when he was alive—he certainly wouldn't do it in death. Hell, Alex, the house was willed to Shelley, not me."

"But you have it."

"I *bought* it. I took out a loan and had to buy my own house from my sister-in-law." Scathing words accompanied a dark flash of disgust in her eyes.

He clenched a fist at his side, struggling to match the man she described with the man he knew. "His parents shut you out, too?"

She let out a dry laugh. "He was their golden boy, and we only got along for Drew's sake. I haven't seen or heard from them since the funeral."

Confusion tugged at his brow as he stared at the lake behind her. Finally, he gave up with a shake of his head. "I don't get it. He made it sound like they adored you."

Chin high, she met his imploring gaze defiantly. "Appearances, Alex. The better he looked all the way around, the better his advancement potential. You know how it goes."

"Do you know what you're asking me to believe?" How could he? Drew Sanders gave his *life* to save Alex's. He had Drew's word to back Shelley's claims that Reagan couldn't handle money. "And if it's true, you've been hiding it from me." He let out a disparaging snort. "You could take me to bed, screw me senseless, and you couldn't tell me the truth."

"*I* could screw *you* senseless?" Her voice rose in pitch. "You've been trying to force me into what you think is appropriate behavior, and never once have you stopped to listen! You're not listening now. You've chosen Drew over me. I see where your loyalty lies."

Alex's own fury made him immune to the tear that tracked down her cheek. "Let's talk about loyalty. I beat myself up with guilt over wanting you. You could have stopped today, Reagan. But you didn't. Even when you saw Shelley earlier, you said nothing. We could have left and talked. We could have worked this out." He released her arm and turned for his pickup, pulling his keys out of his pocket.

"You're turning the tables! You planned this whole thing today. If you'd listened to what I've been saying—that I get a say in my life—this wouldn't have happened at all."

"Yeah, well, it did." And he could feel the distance creeping between them as the seconds passed. He'd bared his soul to her. All the while, she'd held back.

Jesus… Glancing around, he took in the faces he recognized: Jacob, Don, others he placed from Colton but couldn't recall their names. Much like Shelley, disapproval etched into their features as they watched Reagan. They'd heard her angry explosion. Maybe they didn't side with Shelley, maybe they did—whatever the case, they judged Reagan unfavorably. Hell, he wouldn't put it past some of them to judge her for spilling the god-awful truth.

Fuck. What the hell was he supposed to do with this?

Nothing. There was nothing he could do. Nothing more to say. "I have to go."

"I see," she mumbled.

He scoffed bitterly. "Don't give me that 'I see' crap. You don't see. Obviously."

Hot color infused her cheeks as she swiped at another tear. "All along, you've been calling the shots. I've been letting you. You've made your decision, and I'm done trying to convince you otherwise. You didn't want this in the first place, and I pushed for it."

He stared at her, torn between what to believe, how to respond. Silence spanned between them, weighty and suffocating. Slowly, his gaze shifted to his pickup. He couldn't continue this conversation. If he tried, he'd say something he could never take back. What she wanted him to believe contradicted every truth he understood.

She broke the ominous silence, her voice low and flat. "You need to get your stuff out of my house tomorrow morning."

God, just hearing the words felt like he was bleeding out. But she was right. He clenched another tight fist as his illusions of happiness shattered at his feet, then he straightened his shoulders. "Fine," he muttered.

"And I'm leaving now." She whirled on her heel, making a beeline toward the edge of the shelter where Chance and Desi watched them.

They ushered her quickly to their car, the slamming of the doors like firing cannons to his heart. As a heavy weight banded around his ribs, he stormed across the grass, heading for his pickup. He had to get out of here. Escape. Sort through the crap in his head. *Death before dishonor.*

Was Reagan right? What if Drew chose death because he'd been dishonorable?

Alex furiously shook off the thought as he climbed into

the cab and slammed the door. Not Drew. He was the best damn marine Alex knew. Everything he understood about the man couldn't be false. Hell, he'd asked Alex to look after Reagan.

As he fired the engine, he surveyed the people gathered beneath the shelter. No one rose to her defense. Not even Chance and Desi *said* anything to refute her claims, though their support was obvious enough in their actions. Why? Because they knew things about Reagan he didn't?

Or because no one possessed the courage to condemn a Purple Heart awardee?

Looking at you too long.

Christ, *if* what she claimed were true, then he held just as much responsibility for those damned scars. Every time she looked at him must have reminded her of that torture. Maybe that's why she'd clammed up about Drew. Maybe *he* brought her tangible pain. Jesus, that put him on a whole new level of undeserving.

Fuck.

Alex jammed his foot on the gas. Rocks sprayed as he peeled out of the parking lot. He didn't know where he was going, but he sure as hell couldn't stay here and pretend to be normal. Everything he thought he understood just turned on end.

And with it, he'd lost the only woman who ever mattered.

Chapter Twenty-Three

No, no, no, no.

Even after several hours at Desi and Chance's home, the disastrous afternoon well behind her, Reagan still felt violently ill each time Alex's devastated face flashed through her memory. In no way had she planned to spit out the truth as coldly as she just had. She hadn't eased him into the conversation, she'd fucking crushed him in one, unthinking, angry outburst.

Her heart lodged in her throat, and she blinked back tears all over again. Through her back porch door, she glimpsed the warm inviting light spilling onto the grass from Desi's screened-in patio. If she went back there, she could forget with more wine.

But forgetting would only be temporary. In the morning, she'd still have to face that Alex had turned against her. Wine solved nothing. She needed the clarity that would come with morning, and that meant braving the bed that waited. A cold, empty bed, no longer the safe haven it had once been.

Forcing herself to rise out of the overstuffed armchair, she trudged to the stairs.

What else could she do? She'd let the whole mess grow out of control. She'd known the truth would tear them apart, only she hadn't expected it would hurt so damned bad. That when he walked out of her life, he'd take a part of her with him.

Because somewhere along the way, she'd foolishly fallen in love with him.

Love.

She pushed open her bedroom door, crossed to the bed, and flopped stomach-first onto the mattress. A mirthless chuckle escaped her lips as she rolled over and stared at the ceiling, refusing to acknowledge the pillow beside her head and the scent of Alex's skin that clung to the sheets.

Thankfully she hadn't confided the little tidbit that she'd fallen in love. He would have likely thrown it in her face, too. He certainly didn't share the same emotion. If he did, he would have listened, would have known she couldn't make something so ugly up.

She should have been better prepared for his decision. The bonds of soldiers were the bonds of brothers. She shouldn't have been surprised he'd honor Drew's memory until the last. Hell, he owed his life to Drew. She couldn't begin to compete with that. And she wouldn't.

Still, she'd hoped. Prayed that Alex would take her into his arms, hold her tight, and tell her everything would be all right between them.

But he hadn't.

She sniffed back the tears and closed her eyes. Like someone shoved a spike between her ribs, pain flared anew in her chest. So intense her lungs cinched together, and she struggled to find air. He hadn't even *tried* to consider what she had to say. That he was so unwilling to fight for them, fight for the happiness they'd found, only proved he wasn't invested in a future together. *Once a soldier, always a soldier.*

Parting was probably for the best. He'd shown his true colors. Hints bled through in the way he took control of her porch, and she should have seen those signs for what they were. In the end, he proved himself every bit as unbending as Drew. And if he didn't go, she would have begged him to stay. While they'd had a great time, while he made her feel things she'd forgotten could exist, he never got it, never understood her. He bulldozed his way time and again, flexing his control. If he couldn't let go enough to see her as an equal partner, all the love in the world wouldn't make them a *couple*.

But damn it, he wasn't entirely like Drew, and she knew that in the depths of her being. He'd made her feel alive and cherished. Made her laugh. Put her back together again without ever realizing she was broken. And tomorrow, he'd come to her house for his things, only to walk out forever.

Maybe he'd realize this wasn't completely her mess. Maybe he'd acknowledge his own fault and come back full of apologies. Maybe they could somehow...

Her thoughts clogged on a rush of heartbreak. She was fooling herself. He'd already made his choice.

Do not cry, damn it.

The tears betrayed her orders and slid steadily down her cheeks. Wiping them away, she turned her head to gaze out at the starless sky. There were no answers written in those fathomless depths. Just a vast emptiness that gnawed at her soul.

She'd survived before. Picked herself up and put life back together. She could do it again. She might go to her grave loving Alex, but he wouldn't destroy her. She could face the emptiness, rise above it. And somehow, some way, she would.

Chapter Twenty-Four

It was after midnight when Alex managed to pull himself together and move off the bank of the stream north of Colton. Base gut reaction put him on the run, initially urging him back to Chicago. But as he'd crossed the bridge twenty miles south of the lake, something drew him toward Colton, like an invisible thread tying him to Reagan.

He trudged up the bank, his thoughts still as jumbled as when he sat down hours ago. The answer lay just beyond his reach—he could feel it like a tangible thing in his periphery. And yet, no matter how he searched, how he tried to grasp and hold on, it eluded him. Drew. An abuser.

The idea was as dumbfounding as Reagan being a liar.

Maybe talking to her would help.

Of course it would.

He opened his truck door, climbed inside, and started the engine. Now that his shock had worn off and his anger faded somewhat, he stood a better chance of hearing what she *really* said. Talking would be the best for the both of them, and contrary to his outburst, he wasn't ready to give up all they'd discovered these past few days. If there was an iota of hope left, he had to try.

The scant miles passed more quickly than he would have liked, making it impossible to prepare what he wanted to say. When he pulled into her drive, nerves tangled his insides. Her house was dark, not even a solitary lamp burning in the front room. Knocking would wake her up. Once again, he'd be doing exactly what she claimed—thinking only of himself.

Nevertheless, this was about *them*, and they needed to sort it out.

Still, his hand hesitated on the truck door handle. He studied her front porch, not seeing the destruction from the storm but the quaint, shaded overhang that had caught his eye the first time he visited Drew's home. A wind chime had hung on the far corner, its whimsical melody alluring in the late-summer breeze. Little pixie-like fairies sat atop the thin pipes, and he'd been struck by the thought Reagan resembled those magical creatures. Her laughter at the lake, the impish way she sneaked up behind him and dumped a cooler of ice over his head—

Alex's thoughts screeched to a halt. The lake.

Reagan had worn a red, white, and blue bikini. It hung low on her hips, showing off a smooth, flat belly. The sexy little top emphasized the fullness of her breasts, and its ties dangled down her back.

Her smooth, tanned, and unblemished back.

The next afternoon, when he'd come here for dinner, she'd worn a shapeless old T-shirt that struck him as comfortable.

She'd been wearing those same uninspiring T-shirts ever since.

Son of a bitch.

His gut churned violently, and he swallowed down the bitter taste of bile. The man he owed his life to had beaten the crap out of her. Not just with fists—Alex presumed those were involved as well, but didn't really want to know—but with the buckle end of a belt. Hard enough to scar her.

And he'd stake his soul on the fact that the first time had been after the lake.

Drew, an abuser. It was like he'd never really known his best friend. In a thousand years, he never would have dreamed it was possible. Never would have believed Reagan and he were anything but happily married. Truth to tell, if he hadn't witnessed the scars, he might not have believed it still.

But he *had* seen them.

Worse, he'd *caused* them.

Maybe not all of them, but part of them, and the idea that he'd brought her pain, however unwittingly, was even more difficult to accept than the fact that the man who'd been nothing but honorable as a best friend and brother was a shit husband. The idea of Reagan hurting cut Alex like glass.

He dropped his head to the steering wheel with a groan. What had he done in return? Doubted her. All but accused her of lying. All this time she'd been hiding the scars—all the numerous times she'd made a point of staying in the dark, of refusing to show her back when they were intimate, of wearing T-shirts to sleep in after an incredible bout of sex.

All this time he'd ignored her signs.

For God's sake, he'd thought he was a reminder of

Drew—he was. A *painful* reminder.

What to say? How to make it right? Could it ever be *right* again? She had every right to throw him out.

Fuck! He squeezed his eyes shut tight to block the barrage. He was fooling himself—he couldn't do this. He didn't have the right. The pale white scars flashed through his mind, and he cringed. There was no way he could take away that pain. Jesus, he had *caused* it.

Once again, his world was wheeling.

He lifted his head, seeing the house in a different light. How many times had she screamed inside this house? Who had heard her, other than Chance and Desi? Why had no one come to her rescue?

What the fuck had happened to the guy who saved puppies and threw himself on a grenade?

But Alex knew the answer—Drew made a good soldier. Drastically different from being a good man.

He wasn't any shining example, either. Certainly not after today. All along he'd wanted to help her. In the end, he'd failed her utterly.

Jesus, this was too much to cope with. They *couldn't* ever be normal again. She'd never forgive him. She needed a hero, a man who would make her happy, not some jackass bent on having his way. And for the life of him, he didn't know how she could ever tolerate his touch when he must likely remind her of that life.

No, there was no future here. He had no right to that happiness.

He jammed the truck into reverse and backed out of her drive. He'd go home tomorrow. The clothes he'd bought at the hardware store weren't worth the heartache retrieving them would bring.

At the edge of town, a blue and white sign lit up Colton's only hotel, and he pulled into the lot. It took a handful of minutes to obtain lodging from the kid behind the desk. After paying for a night's stay, he let himself inside the stuffy little room and sank onto the edge of the bed. Head hanging in his hands, he fought back a riptide of stifling emotion. Damn it. The last thing on earth he wanted to do was leave Reagan. But he couldn't see a way to forge the divide that spanned between them. He wanted to kill his best friend all over again. And yet, he didn't know how to move beyond the fact that Reagan hadn't trusted him with the truth.

Because it was his fault. He'd pushed and pushed, convinced he knew what was best for her.

A bitter snort slipped free, and he lay back against the pillows. The whole damned mess was his fault. From Drew's death, to this. Some fucking hero he was. He could have given her everything she needed, could have proven himself.

Instead, he acted just like Shelley.

Now, he was even considering bailing like a coward. No...he had to go to her house tomorrow. Had to see her one last time. It would be torture. Looking at her and actually saying good-bye... If he managed to get through it without falling to his knees in tears, he'd be amazed. And that would be embarrassing as hell. He certainly didn't want her parting memory to be him as a soggy, weak mess.

But leaving her was like the final nail in a suffocating coffin. He'd lost everything—his best friend, the woman he loved, good friends he'd made in the marines, and now, even his sense of self to some degree.

The woman he loved? He stumbled over the realization,

his heart wrenching again. Yeah, he did. Loved her beyond reason. How the hell it had happened, he couldn't say, but he'd fucked it up astronomically, and now he felt…empty. Anxiety strangely lurked beneath that nothingness. His head was a mess, but somewhere, behind all the racket in his brain, he knew his solace would come with her. Just like he knew safety lay outside of the hut that had trapped Drew and him, but he couldn't find a way to get there in time. Now, he didn't know how to meet Reagan in that out-of-reach place.

Or even if he deserved her. How many more times would he cause her pain without realizing it, because he was too damn dense to read her signs?

Screw it. He'd get his things and walk away. Reagan deserved better. She would find her hero, find her happiness. And she couldn't with him standing in the way.

Chapter Twenty-Five

Alex woke to bright sunlight. Silence blanketed him, save for the muted call of an owl. He stared at the ceiling, on the cusp of something he couldn't fully comprehend, but it rushed through his veins with the same spike of adrenaline that came with being stuck in a foxhole with bullets whizzing overhead.

Reagan expected him to get his things and leave today. He could do so and be out of Colton before she woke.

No. That wouldn't happen.

Oh, he'd be gone when she woke, but he—*they*—weren't done yet. His shock had passed. The truth lay before him. His best friend had been a bastard of a husband. Shelley turned on Reagan, and judging from the reaction of half the town yesterday, Reagan's closed-off nature garnered her few allies. Only a coward would walk out of Colton and leave her to suffer that isolation.

He might be many things, but he wasn't a coward. He'd

damaged her enough; now he needed to fix it. Make apologies the best he could before wishing her well and giving her the wings to find happiness. With or without him.

He swung his legs off the motel room bed and fished his keys out of his pocket. She'd be pissed as hell when afternoon rolled around and he showed up on her doorstep, but this time, when she ordered him to leave, he'd be ready. He could go back to Chicago with no regrets. She needed a hero, and while he didn't possess a Purple Heart, he had a medal or two under his belt. Maybe lending them to her for a little bit would cool some of her fire. He doubted it, but hell, he was born to fight. And fight he would. For her.

He crossed to the door and yanked it open. Goddamn Drew. Goddamn Shelley.

The woman in that neglected house across town should be applauded. For the silence she maintained and the secrets she kept—no doubt to preserve Drew's honor. For the strength and resilience she possessed. For fighting a battle that had to have been more damaging than anything Alex experienced on the field. *She* was the real hero, and it was about time Colton took note of it.

He tossed his bags into his pickup, then slid behind the wheel. Seven in the morning. The hardware store opened at eight. Small towns had gathering places, where the old guard could often be found for breakfast and coffee. Don most assuredly held an old guard card.

Alex slammed the truck into reverse and peeled out of the parking lot. He'd start there, where a man's reputation could be shattered or memorialized in a single utterance.

He drove into the heart of Colton, past the Cock 'n' Bull, to the oldest quarter of town. A dingy sign hung over one bricked-in doorway, faded letters reading Mo's BAKERY. COFFEE. BREAKFAST.

Alex parked in the first open spot he found and jumped out of his pickup. Saying a silent prayer that he'd made the right guess—though, really, Colton didn't have much else to offer—he strode confidently through the door. A bell tinkled, announcing his entrance. From behind a wide counter that screamed 1960, a gray-haired woman greeted him with a cordial smile. To the left of the display case, eight men gathered around a long table. Don dipped his head, acknowledging Alex as well.

He returned the short nod and approached the counter. "Cinnamon roll, please, and a cup of black coffee."

"Of course. You're Alex McCray, aren't you? Served with Drew Sanders, right?"

Resisting the gut response to grind his teeth, he forced a smile. "Yes, ma'am."

A speculative light glinted behind her smile, telling Alex exactly what he suspected—word had spread of yesterday's picnic. Reagan's explosion knocked her down a few more pegs in their eyes. He bit back a flicker of annoyance.

When she returned with his order, he tossed a few bills on the counter to cover the cost and provide a decent tip, then turned and marched straight for the secluded group in the corner.

Don looked up, startled. "McCray. Morning."

Noticeably, no one offered the empty chair. Alex hooked it with the toe of his boot and pulled it out. He took a seat and sipped from his coffee. "Morning, Don. You know what time the VFW opens?" Glancing around the small table, he took in the faces. Aging men, some a good decade older than the others. They all had the air, the presence Alex associated with servicemen. That little bit of piety combined with good ol' down-home warmth. He'd stake his entire retirement that every one of these men had served at some point or another.

Don motioned to the man across from him, a graying, freckled man with a full white beard. "Hank, what time are you opening it up today?"

"Well, that depends," he drawled. "Jeannie says I've got to mow the grass." He cocked his head at Alex. "You need something, son?"

"Actually, I do." Alex took another drink from his cup, and then set it aside. He tore off a hunk of cinnamon roll. "But I think I can accomplish it here." He popped the bite into his mouth, chewed, and took his time surveying the men. "There's a lady in need on the north side of town. A teacher, probably to your grandkids."

The table shifted as a collective unit, each man clearly uncomfortable as their focus dropped to their mugs.

"Seems she married a soldier. A marine. And his marine family isn't doing right by her, now that he's dead."

Don cleared his throat. He turned his coffee mug between long, tapered fingers. "What are you getting at, son?"

Alex held his gaze. "I don't know about you, Don, but I swore myself to the creed, 'Death before Dishonor.' Yet I see a whole lot of dishonoring going on."

"Now, wait a damn minute," the man to Don's left barked. "You don't mean to tell me you believe that young man who gave his life protecting his team would come home and knock his wife around. We never saw any evidence of it."

Fire lighted in Alex's veins. The pure, instinctual need to

stand up and fight for right. He thumped the flat of his hand onto the table, making coffee cups jump. "Drew Sanders was my best friend. He died, not protecting his team, but protecting *me* because I made a bad call. And I'll tell you now, without a doubt, he beat his wife. With a goddamn belt. She's got more honor than any one of us at this table. She kept his secret. Left you to your hero fantasies. And what does she get in return? Her integrity drawn through the mud."

"Easy, son," Don said calmly.

Alex pushed himself out of his seat. Hands still braced on the table, he bent over the men. "There's no easy to it. Even if you've said nothing, you've condemned her. And it's past time someone does what's right. She needs your help. You"—he pointed at Don—"have supplies." He nodded at the man next to him. "And you've probably got a son who can wield a hammer." He shifted his gaze to the man to his right, a heavyset quiet man with old-fashioned wire-rimmed glasses. "And you—do you have a son or daughter?"

The man nodded uneasily. "My son's thirty-two tomorrow."

Alex shook his head sadly. "And where was he when the tree fell on Reagan's house?"

Color raced into the man's face, all the way to the top of his balding head. He dropped his gaze to his plate. Shifted uncomfortably in his seat.

"All right, you've made your point." Don leaned back in his chair and chewed on the inside of his cheek. "Did you come in here today to shame us like mangy dogs, or did you have something else to say?"

Drawing in a deep breath of air, Alex pushed down his temper and lowered himself into his seat. He plucked off another bite of his roll, chewed it slowly. When he swallowed it down, he folded his hands in front of him and eyed every man in turn. "I want that tree out of her house. I want that porch put back on, exactly like it was. Down to the nail holes. I want her windows fixed, and I want you all to make it happen. I'm not a hero. No more than any of you. But if this town is so intent on seeing me as one, you tell me where to throw my medals around. Because I'll give every goddamn one of them away to undo what she's suffered."

The burliest man of the group leaned forward from his tucked-away position in the corner. He fixed Alex with a narrowed gaze. "He was a Purple Heart awardee."

Alex ground his teeth together and slowly curled a hand into a fist.

But he didn't have to say a word. Don leaned forward as well, resting his elbows on the table and leveling his friend with a hard look. "You know what war does to men, Chuck."

Chuck opened his mouth as if he intended to protest, then quickly snapped it shut. He leaned back in his chair with a mutter.

Don turned to Alex. "That wall has to come off her house. There's no use putting that porch back on until it's replaced. You can cut out trees, you can tack on shingles, you can tear down porches, but it's only a Band-Aid."

Alex pushed away from the table and rose to his feet. "I trust you know how to see about getting that done." He strode away, burying the smile that tried to break free. He'd succeeded. They would come. Maybe not today. Maybe not tomorrow. But they would come.

He wouldn't see it—once he told Reagan what he'd done, any chance of ever fixing things would be ruined.

Once more, he'd taken control out of her hands, and damn sure she wouldn't realize this time it was necessity. She could speak until she was blue in the face, and no one would have listened. Alex wouldn't have accomplished anything either, if he hadn't faced a group of veterans and condemned his best friend. Those men knew loyalty, and they knew what it took to turn away.

. . .

Reagan descended the stairs for the third time. She knew what she'd find in the living room — emptiness, his abandoned clothes only a mere trace Alex had ever slept there, ever occupied space in her house. But each time she entered, pain stabbed anew, as if she looked on everything for the first time. Half the day had passed, and she'd managed to find energy only to water her sapling in the front yard.

The rest of the time, she attempted to work on lesson plans, but ideas remained lodged behind a veil of sorrow she couldn't penetrate.

It was better this way. Better they say good-bye than become even more tangled together where she lost her sense of self. Her control over her life. But a little voice nagged that he hadn't oppressed her. Everything came from his heart. Driven by the need to help her. And like the other little slips she'd suffered, she'd mistaken him for Drew and backtracked to a different time and place.

A different man.

She sank into the armchair with a sigh and stared at the couch where they'd first made love. A wry chuckle slipped free as she considered the air-conditioner. Top of the line.

Energy efficient. Who in their right mind criticized that?

She'd told him to go. Really ended everything.

If only she could take it all back.

A chainsaw fired beyond her window. Blinking, Reagan hurried to the window. Maybe he'd come back. Maybe…

Dismay drooped her shoulders. Not Alex. Kenneth Yardsley's son David stood beneath what remained of her broken tree. Chance must have phoned him. And if that wasn't proof Reagan had overreacted with Alex, she didn't know what was. She never threw fits when Chance stepped in. She owed Alex the same gratitude and courtesy she gave her best friend's husband.

Rattling at the front door brought her around with a frown. But before she could answer, it swung open. Alex stepped inside.

Reagan's breath caught, and she couldn't tear her eyes away. He filled up the doorway, his broad shoulders nearly spanning the full width. He wore the same clothes he had yesterday, but with the afternoon sunlight spilling in behind him, he looked more handsome than ever before. Oh, dear God, her heart raced out of control. "Alex?" she whispered.

He set two large sacks over the back of the couch and gave her an awkward smile. "I dropped in to confess my sins."

Her brow bunched in puzzlement. "What?"

With a tip of his head, he acknowledged the revving motor outside. "I arranged for him to come. Someone else will handle the rest of the porch demolition and reconstruction." His gaze held hers, uncertainty reflecting in the deep green depths. "It needed to be done, and I can't finish it."

"Can't?" She hesitated, then blurted, "Or won't?"

Alex shook his head. "I don't know how to finish what's

left." He tapped one sack. "Parts. Hardware. I don't think you'll need anything else. And I know you don't like me making decisions for you, but…" He blew out a hard breath. "This time, I don't really care. You need it."

Her heart tripped at the sudden emotion that reflected in his quiet stare. Once again, he'd done this for her. Out of goodness. Out of tenderness. "Alex—"

"No, I don't want hear it." The muscles alongside his jaw ticked. "You deserve it, Reagan. And I'm leaving, because I know I just did the same damn thing you screamed at me about. The same damn thing Drew did over and over. I couldn't fix it then, but I can fix this. I refuse—"

"It's not the same."

He stopped, mid-sentence, a sharp intake of air hissing between his teeth.

Reagan didn't wait for him to respond. Twisting her hands at her waist, she rushed into words. "I slipped. I flashed back, and I only now realized what I was doing. You aren't Drew, and everything you've done is priceless. I'm sorry I accused you of being like him. We're both human. We make mistakes." She hesitated a moment, then drew in a deep gulp of air. "Don't go. Please."

Chapter Twenty-Six

Goddamn. Every logical response fled Alex's brain. He couldn't have spoken if he wanted to—her apology rendered him thunderstruck. With a shake of his head, he stalked to where she stood and kissed her hard. The fist behind his ribs let go, granting him a small amount of air. He breathed deeply, pulled back, and exhaled shakily. He rested his forehead against hers, eyes closed. "Oh, fuck, Reagan. Why didn't you tell me? Why did you stay with him? I'd have helped you. I'd have…" His throat tightened around emotion. Giving up on speech, he threaded his fingers into her hair and held her close.

Her words whispered through the silence. "I was young. I was nineteen, and he swept me off my feet. I was dying to escape my junkie folks, so I ran with him. Those first few months were good. Then he enlisted. When the abuse started, I didn't have anywhere to go."

He couldn't help but grimace.

Reagan ran her hand up his back affectionately and then continued. "Then there was school. As long as I was married, I had tuition benefits. I told myself I could deal with the bad because it would pay off in the end. And then, there's a period where you question maybe you've deserved the fists, maybe you've caused them."

"No," he said, roughly.

She pulled back and shook her head. "I'm past that now, Alex. But you asked why I stayed."

Reluctantly, he encouraged her with a nod. He wasn't certain he wanted to hear the rest, but he'd asked, and he supposed, on some level, he *needed* to hear.

With a huffed sigh, she blew the hair out of her face. "Then Drew was gone most of the time, and I had a new job. I thought maybe counseling might take us back to where we were once. But his noose kept tightening—cutting me off financially, cutting me off socially. I had my salary, but I had no home if I left. My paycheck went into a joint account and changing that would have made things worse. Up and running away wasn't an option. I *love* my job. Love the kids here in Colton. So I was secretly saving to make that break. Which wasn't easy, because he knew exactly how much I made, and I could only set back small amounts. Chance and Desi slipped me money when they could, much as my pride hated that. In the end, when Drew died, they co-signed on the house loan for me."

So they *had* helped her. A measure of relief he hadn't anticipated flowed through him. Maybe they hadn't intervened, but maybe there wasn't an easy way to assist. Maybe anything they might have tried to do would have only made things worse for Reagan—particularly if their efforts failed.

He studied her serene expression. She was so pretty, so heartbreakingly genuine as she stared into his eyes, unblinking. And he ached to touch her. To taste the sweetness of her kiss. To feel her soft skin brushing against his.

He reached for her, sliding one arm around her waist. The other wrapped around her shoulders, enveloping her against his body. He smoothed a hand down her back, closed his eyes.

And felt the damned scars against his fingertips through the light material of her T-shirt.

Fuck.

Grimacing at the pain he could never take from her, he refused the instinct to release her and leaned back to look into her eyes. *I love you.*

Anguish twisted his mouth. His words came out broken and thick. "I want to touch you so badly, but I all I see is…"

"My scars," she finished for him.

He nodded, hating the ugly truth of it all.

She set a shaky palm against his cheek. "That's all they are, Alex. Scars. Not open wounds. You have them, too." Reaching between them, she clasped his hand and pressed it to her breast. "Love me. The way I love you."

Love him. A shudder gripped him so hard he fought to stay standing. He was shaking all over, never more desperate to touch a woman. Beneath his fingertips, Reagan's flesh was warm and soft. He could feel her steady heartbeat. Feel the brush of her breath against his knuckles as she exhaled. Sheer instinct overruled all thought, and he gently kneaded his fingertips against her breast. "I would die before I hurt you," he whispered hoarsely.

She covered his hand with hers. "I know. I know it in my

heart, in my soul."

He swallowed down the hard lump that lodged in the back of his throat, and licked his lips to moisten them. "I want to love you, Reagan, and I don't ever want to stop."

One tear trickled down her cheek. "Then do. I'm right here, waiting."

Something inside him broke. Maybe the wall he'd erected. Maybe something deeper and more critical—he wasn't certain. But he felt the rip and tear as surely as he felt the uptick of her heartbeat. He brought his fingers toward her face, holding his breath as he sought to brush away her tears, afraid she'd twist away.

She didn't. Instead, she turned her cheek into his hand and rubbed it against his palm. He cupped the side of her face and drew his thumb over her lips. She met the gentle caress with a soft kiss. Slowly, hesitantly, he bent his head, knowing the minute his lips touched hers there would be no turning back. But he needed the safe harbor that lay in her arms. Needed the absolution she offered.

Her mouth dusted across his. Longing pulled through him like a thread drawn from the soles of his feet out through his chest. Heaven lurked in the sweet tangle of her tongue, and it called to him with a promise of salvation. He gave in, bringing his other hand up to frame her face between his palms.

At the stroke of her tongue, another shudder racked him, this one more powerful than the last, as every remaining defense crumbled away. She had him. All of him. And he could no longer fight the yearning in his soul. He no longer had to. He dropped a hand to her waist, wound it around her, and drew her against his body. Contentment poured through his veins as her softness melded into him. This was right. So very right.

Hunger stirred to life, the craving for all that she was and all she had to give. Along with the need to give everything he was. He skimmed his hands to her waist and tugged up the fitted T-shirt she wore. When it caught on her arms, he ended the kiss to look into her eyes. "Turn around."

Hesitation reflected in her blue eyes, uncertainty and apprehension. But she didn't refuse like she had before. She dropped her gaze and reluctantly presented her back. Alex gently pulled her shirt off and dropped it at her feet.

In the warm afternoon light, the scars across her upper back held a silvery sheen. The sight of them cut him to the quick all over again, and he drew in a deep, steadying breath. He couldn't take them from her, couldn't undo her suffering. He had to accept that. Had to accept them.

"Alex," Reagan protested uncomfortably. "Please, there's no need. There are people—"

She broke off on a sharp gasp as he covered one horseshoe mark with his mouth and shifted her ever so slightly beyond the line of sight from the window. He kissed her softly at first, testing his own comfort as much as hers with the brush of his lips. When a tremor raced through her body and she went pliant in his arms, he parted his lips and traced the raised flesh with the tip of his tongue.

The ridges and bumps were like tiny pokers thrust into his heart. He closed his eyes, absorbing the pain, pushing through it as he moved from one mark to another, until it was no longer an intolerable ache, but a bittersweet pleasure. Tiny shudders made her tremble. The soft gasps that fell from her lips punctured his soul, filling him so full, his heart swelled to overflowing.

God, what she'd gone through. Somehow, some way, he would make all that right. Replace every bit of her hurt with far more pleasant memories.

He dropped his hands to the waistband of her shorts and slid them around, taking his lips off her skin only long enough to unfasten the denim and push it down her hips. It joined the shirt on the floor. Then he moved lower, tracing still more scars, lost to the sheer enjoyment of knowing her more intimately than he'd ever dreamed was possible. And it was intimate, this simple foreplay. So personal and penetrating that his eyes misted over.

But he couldn't stop the riptide of emotion, and before it could consume him completely, he banded an arm around her waist, bent her in against his body, and with a low groan dragged his chin up her spine to plant an openmouthed kiss at the base of her neck. Her bottom fit against his groin, awakening a deeper, more primitive hunger. Fully nude, her body heat soaked through his jeans. With one heavy thump of his heart, his cock filled to capacity.

He arched his hips, pressing into the sensitive flesh beneath her buttocks, letting her know just how much he wanted her.

Reagan answered with another soft gasp and a rock of her pelvis that stroked him so perfectly tiny sparks of light danced across the backs of his eyelids. He lifted his head as he slid one hand up her belly to cup her breast. "God, Reagan, the things you do to me," he rasped through his labored breathing.

She leaned back against him, resting her head on his shoulder. Subtly, she canted her hips again, a side-to-side shimmy that only made him want to bend her over the couch and slam home again and again. Yet he fought the base urge, in need of something deeper, more meaningful.

"Come upstairs?" she asked.

"If we go now, we might make it there." He dragged his teeth down the side of her throat. "Otherwise, it's the couch again."

With a light giggle, she glided out of his arms and captured his hand. "No couch. The bed's softer." She rose on tiptoe and placed a lingering kiss full of promise on his lips. "And when we're too exhausted to move, we don't have to."

He was so on board with that plan. Taking over the lead, he led her up the stairs in double time.

Inside her room, Reagan seated herself on the edge of the mattress and dipped her fingers into the waistband of his jeans. With quick, nimble fingers, she bared him completely. Then that delectable mouth wafted across his navel, bringing every nerve ending to life. His cock bobbed, nudging against her chin.

"Someone's antsy," she murmured a heartbeat before she dipped the tip of her tongue into his belly button.

"Um. Yeah." He couldn't find any other words, to his chagrin. The warmth of her breath, so devastatingly close to his erection, stripped him senseless.

Reagan noticed his moment of dysfunction and laughed softly. "What's the matter, Alex? Cat got your tongue?"

He arched an eyebrow, searching for a retort, but before he could come up with anything, her tongue danced over the swollen head of his cock. Heat seared into his bloodstream, and he gripped her shoulders to keep his knees from buckling. She looked up at him through her eyelashes, the hint of a smile on her mouth.

"How's this?" she whispered before her lips closed around him.

Alex's eyes went wide at the pressure of her mouth. He tried to inhale and managed nothing but a sharp, short gasp through the enormous pleasure. On a groan, he slid one hand to the side of her face and stroked her cheek with his thumb. "Fuck, that's perfect," he rasped.

She took him deeper, swirling her tongue against his shaft as she glided along him. His body tensed, the urge to push farther, to feel her throat constricting as she swallowed him down, pounding at him. But he held back, giving her control. Later he'd indulge. Much later. Right now...

Her teeth scraped against him, and Alex's breathing became more labored. Climax rose steadily, each suck, each slide, bringing it closer to the surface. His cock pulsed against the back of her mouth. And Reagan opened a little wider, swallowing him down, drowning him in perfect pleasure. Against his will, his body moved, pushing deeper, pulling away only to sink once more. Her gaze lifted again, brilliant blue imprisoning him. The trust that glinted in those heavenly depths pushed him to the razor's edge. Gasping hard, he pulled completely out of her mouth and wrapped a fist around his cock to tame his over-sensitized nerve endings.

Reagan slid a delicate palm up his thigh. "You could have—"

Not yet able to speak, Alex cut her off with an adamant shake of his head. He wanted every damn bit of her. He gestured at the bed with his free hand.

Following his cue, Reagan lay back on the mattress. He took another moment to pull himself back from the precipice of ecstasy before kneeling between her spread knees and levering himself onto his hands. His gaze strayed down her body, drinking her in from her high and full breasts, to the narrow juncture of her hips, to the strawberry blond curls between her legs.

Fuck. He was fooling himself—he might want to indulge in her all damn day, but there was no way his body would cooperate with that idea. The sight of his cock nestled against her feminine folds had him right back on the edge, release pounding at his senses. He dropped his head to her shoulder with a quiet grunt. "You have no idea how much I want to take my time. But I'm afraid that isn't going to happen."

Reagan's hands slid up his biceps, and she arched her back, guiding the tip of his cock inside her wet flesh. "I think I'd complain if you did." She lifted higher, drawing him inside more fully. "Take me, Alex. Make love to me. Please."

When he pushed into her, they both groaned. He sought her mouth and kissed her as he sank deeper and deeper. Her inner walls contracted around him, gripping and squeezing, drawing him in farther until he was buried completely. And yet he needed more. He tore his mouth away. "Wrap your legs around my waist."

Reagan obeyed, twisting beneath him, her movements as desperate as the need searing through his veins. The soft little whimpers that escaped her parted lips as they pushed against each other obliterated the shreds of control he clung to. He gave in to it, in to the passion she pulled from deep inside him, and allowed himself to become lost in her.

Frenzied hands tangled, their mouths clashed and parted, only to seek each other yet again with another hard, frantic kiss. Each thrust wasn't enough, and yet, somehow more fulfilling than the last. It was too much, too overwhelming, too…all consuming. He needed to slow down, to hang on just a moment longer.

"Slower, baby," he murmured.

But he was already coming, spilling into her uncontrollably, and so was she, her body milking him dry with every mind-searing pulse of her flesh.

Chapter Twenty-Seven

Alex, once again, woke before Reagan and cursed his internal clock. The sun had barely poked through the stars, and he couldn't remember ever being so sated. All he wanted to do was curl up beside her, sleep in until noon, and repeat yesterday and last night all over again. Three times, he'd made love to her. Three times he'd sworn he couldn't know greater pleasure, and yet, he'd found it with each release. He'd indulged like he'd wanted to, taking his time and loving her thoroughly, then waking for another desperate, hungry round. And finally, *finally,* when the emotion ebbed to a bearable level and need gave way to more playful indulgences, he'd rolled her onto her belly and taken her from behind, at last able to lick, bite, touch, and squeeze her glorious ass to his heart's content.

She'd let him, too. No ounce of hesitation, no trace of apprehension, clung to her when she knelt on all fours, caged beneath him as his body dominated hers. Trust flowed between them more tangible than the perspiration on their bodies. He'd made love to those scars with his mouth while he made love to the rest of her.

Bathing in the memories, Alex lifted to one elbow and smoothed a hand down her bare spine. Spread out on her stomach beside him, she slept like an angel. And God, it was nice to wake up to her naked instead of covered in a damned T-shirt.

The air-conditioner kicked on, filling the house with a quiet, soothing hum. In that moment, Alex noticed the silence in his head. The chaos was gone. The questions answered somewhere between her sweet, intoxicating kisses. No more Drew haunting his conscience, no more questioning Reagan's actions. She was strong in ways he couldn't fully fathom, and that strength only made him love her more. In some strange, unexplainable way, she'd shattered his world, only to sew it together more tightly than before. He was done fucking around. No more doubting himself. She'd offered him absolution, and it was time to take a leap of faith and make the commitment, wherever it led. If he'd read the affection in her eyes last night right, he had a firm suspicion it would lead to old age and wheelchairs. Maybe a couple of kids to look after them in their golden years.

Heavy banging on the front door filtered through his awareness. Crap. He'd told her he'd made arrangements for her house…but he hadn't quite confessed to everything. Their conversation took a drastically different course yesterday. And now there wasn't time. He refused to wake her after keeping her up through the night.

He pressed a kiss to her shoulder, over one of the silvery marks, and hurried out of bed. He suspected he'd pay for this later. But he chose to have faith she wouldn't be unreasonable.

God help him—he hoped he was right.

As quietly as possible, he dressed and slipped out of her room, careful to shut the door behind him soundlessly. Then, as the first birds greeted the morning, he opened the front door to find Chance and Don standing on the broken porch.

Chance eyed him warily. "You sure this is a good idea?"

No, he wasn't sure at all. But when Don had followed him out of the bakery, one thing led to another. In less than a half hour, plans were laid. Phone calls made. Alex couldn't have stopped the momentum if he wanted to. Not that he did.

"Sure," he answered nonchalantly. "I told her I made arrangements for the house."

Chance quirked an eyebrow. "She didn't hand you your balls?"

Don chuckled.

A wry grin took up residence on Alex's mouth. "Nope. Still intact."

"Well, I've got the full crew. Where do you want us to start?" Don asked.

· · ·

A loud *thump* yanked Reagan out of sleep. Muscles she didn't even know she possessed protested as she tried to twist out of the tangle of covers. Her eyes felt like someone had tried to glue them shut and didn't want to stay open, so she lolled back into the pillows, convinced she'd dreamed the noise.

Until another loud *thump* had her eyes snapping wide again. This time, she tugged at the quilts until one corner pulled free. Finally able to toss them aside, she slung them back and slid out of the bed. What in the world was Alex doing outside, and after the night they'd had, how could he find the energy?

Wearily, she trudged to the window and pushed aside the thin sheer to gaze down at her front porch. Instead of the half-standing roof, all she saw was two upright posts framing a pile of splintered wood and broken shingles. No Alex in sight. But two strange men filled two wheelbarrows with the debris. Wait—was that Jacob Nance and Mike Owens? What the hell?

Reagan's brow furrowed as a series of muffled, rhythmic *whumps* echoed from the back side of her house. What in the world was going on? It sounded like someone was taking a sledgehammer to the ground. A *giant* one.

When her house actually shook, she let out a squeak and ran to the door. She yanked it half open before she remembered she was naked and bolted back to her closet for a pair of jeans shorts and a tank top. She dragged both on, then dashed out of the room and down the stairs.

She came to an abrupt halt at the bottom of the stairwell. Bright sunlight poured through the front corner of her living room. Not through the window like normal. Through the *ceiling,* which was...missing. At least several feet of the area that didn't support the one-room half story above.

Her mouth fell open. The house shuddered again, and a clump of drywall broke loose from the topmost corner of her front wall, just beneath the gaping hole in the roof. Not trusting she wasn't still dreaming, she backed out of the room into the kitchen, then spun on her heel and bolted out the back patio door.

Only to run smack-dab into David Yardsley. He gave her a crooked grin, tapped the brim of his ball cap, and said, "Sorry to disturb you, Reagan."

Um. Yeah. Where the hell was Alex?

Her gaze darted around her patio, and she counted two additional townspeople, totaling four sons and one daughter of the local veterans tinkering around with her house. The man and woman in the yard drove neon orange-painted garden stakes into the ground between the two beautiful old oaks. Right where she'd planned to put the greenhouse. Was that Chance standing near the far tree?

She blinked twice to clear the rest of the sleep from her vision, then frowned again. Yes, Chance was standing there. Alex stood beside him as Chance pointed to different areas of her lawn.

"Alex?" she asked.

A shout rang out from the side of her house, and no sooner had her voice died off than the engine to some sort of large machinery fired up. Her heart picked up speed as a growing sense of panic spread over her. Alex said he'd made arrangements for what was necessary. She'd pictured a roof that didn't leak, a restored porch, and maybe some new paint. She never would have agreed to this sort of extra extravagance.

She marched across the patio, through the lawn, and came up behind both men. "Excuse me, gentlemen?"

Chance and Alex spun as if a firecracker had exploded behind them.

"Morning, Reagan," Chance quipped, his grin broad and

wide and full of mischief. He shot an uncomfortable-looking Alex a wink, then backed a good three feet away. "I'll be back. Checking on my coffee."

Reagan eyed Alex warily. "What's going on?"

He stubbed a boot-clad toe into the ground with a hesitant smile. "I didn't mean for them to wake you up. I told them to stay quiet."

Something about his sheepish look made him even more adorable, and she had trouble hanging on to her annoyance. She managed to shake her head and train her voice into a flat tone. "Um. Not the problem. Somehow I think this defies *necessary* repairs."

"Well, you see…" He moved closer and clasped both her hands, turning her a half step so she faced the staked-out area in the grass. He looped one arm around her shoulders and pulled her against his side. "It was time to hire someone who knew what the hell they were doing."

She arched an eyebrow. *Don't blow up. He's trying to be helpful.* "Alex," she started calmly, "there's a *hole* in my house. A big hole. And the walls are shaking. And what does the house have to do with this?" She gestured at the orange-tipped stakes.

He shifted his weight, clearly uncomfortable.

Alarms rang in her head. Her gaze narrowed on him with suspicion. "What is it?"

He heaved a hard breath. "It's a bit more complicated than I intended. I wanted the porch fixed, the roof redone, and your window replaced. But when I consulted Don—"

"Don?"

"Yeah, I talked with the members of the VFW. They all agreed it was time to help you out."

Help her out? After the way they'd avoided her since Drew's death? Alex had swayed the prominent members of the town in her favor. Holy cow. The man really could work miracles.

"One thing led to another, and we got to talking about your greenhouse…"

Greenhouse? Reagan blinked at the staked-out spot on the ground as her mind connected the dots. Chance. Alex. Greenhouse. She'd told Chance and Desi her dream in detail. Chance had to have told Alex. Alex was making it happen. Holy shit! He was building her a greenhouse. But… *why?*

"You're taking this better than I expected." He cocked his head and studied her.

Aware she'd missed the rest of what he'd said, she blinked again. "Huh?"

"The house, the front wall—I expected a bit more reaction."

"Wait. What about the house?" She shook off her stunned elation over the greenhouse and glanced back at her home.

Alex cleared his throat. "The whole front wall has to come off."

"Say *what*?" she squeaked. Visions of her entire living room exposed to the elements flashed through her mind. She couldn't afford that kind of repair job. Certainly not this year. "Why?" she demanded. "No." She shook her head violently. "No, you've got to make them stop."

"Sweetheart." He set both hands on her shoulders again, turned her to face him, and dipped his head until his gaze was level with hers. "It has to. The studs cracked under the strain of the tree. You put a new roof on, in four, five years, you're going to have major structural damage as the house settles. That's why your window is broken. The entire exterior wall up to the support for the half story is bowed out."

Reagan let out a groan and buried her face in her hands. "I can't afford that." And the greenhouse—it was like looking at her dream and having to turn away. She certainly didn't have the money to build something *extra* when it would take everything she had to pay off the massive repairs already under way. "Why didn't you consult me?"

"Because I don't want you worrying." He set two fingers under her chin and tipped her head up. "Don's donated a lot of the materials. Everyone volunteered. What we can't do—and there are a couple things that require outside contractors—I've got it covered."

"You...have it...covered?" Dumbfounded, she could only stare. Colton's residents *volunteered* to help rebuild her home. The whole scene was too surreal. If she pinched herself, she was certain she'd realize she was dreaming.

"Yep, and there's not going to be any fuss for you to deal with, either." A touch of self-satisfied pride crept into his voice as his mouth curved with a smile. "We're going to go see some gorillas and big cats. And giraffes. They assure me the repairs to the house will be finished by the time we get back. You can consult with Don before we go and tell him exactly what you want with the greenhouse. He said they might be able to have it finished as well, depending on how many men he can round up."

Reagan's thoughts spun at a dizzying rate. Gorillas. Greenhouse. House repairs. Volunteers from Colton. Alex was doing all this for her. She'd get to design her own greenhouse. Holy cow Africa! But why? Why was he doing all this? It was far more than necessary. She didn't want to be indebted to him, even if they had reached some sort of agreement about their relationship last night. Come to think of it—*had* they reached an agreement?

"Reagan?" he asked, concerned.

"Um."

"Shit," he muttered and massaged the back of his neck with one hand. "You're pissed. I—"

Pulling herself together, she pressed two fingers to his mouth to cut off the direction his thoughts were taking. "No. It's not that." She looked back at the house, then the quartered-off area, then back at Alex. Chewing on her lower lip for a minute, she debated what to say. But the only thing that kept pounding through her mind was why. What did this all mean? Did it mean anything at all?

"Why?" she finally blurted.

"Why?" he echoed, like he couldn't believe she didn't understand. Then his eyes widened, and color crept into his cheeks. "I forgot that part, didn't I?" He cleared his throat again and gathered both her hands once more, holding them loosely between them. "I guess I got a little nervous and left out the most important thing. I love you, Reagan."

A gasp slid from her lips. Before she could fully recover, Alex tipped his head to the side, studying her, the light in his eyes tender and affectionate.

"And you love me, too."

Tears clouded her vision. Alex McCray loved her. *Love.* Her throat entirely too narrow to push sound through, she nodded, vigorously.

Chuckling softly, he took a step back, and still holding

on to her hands, sank to one knee. His words were softer when he spoke, the emotion reflecting in his eyes so warm and bright it made her heart skip several beats.

"I will give you everything I have, everything I am, if you will give me your heart for eternity. Let me take care of you the way you should be, let me love you the way you deserve." He paused, his throat working as he swallowed hard. "Grow old with me, Reagan. Marry me."

Too overcome by emotion to breathe, much less hold herself upright, she sank to her knees with him, nodding so hard she was certain her head would jostle loose.

Alex wrapped her in his arms, feathered a kiss against her hair. He held her tight, his heart thumping steadily against her breast. She clung to him, tears spilling freely down her cheeks as her fingers roamed reverently over the words on his dagger tattoo. He had his answers; she'd made it plain what she wanted. But he'd gone to such lengths that he deserved the spoken promise.

She couldn't manage anything beyond a broken whisper. "I love you, too, Alex." She sniffled, pulling back to give him a watery smile. "And yes. I'll marry you. Just tell me when."

About the Author

National Bestselling Author Tori St. Claire grew up writing. Hobby quickly turned into passion when she discovered the world of romance as a teen. Poems and short stories gave way to full-length novels with sexy heroes and heroines. She wrote her first romance novel at seventeen. While that manuscript gathered dust beneath the bed, she established herself as Claire Ashgrove, an award-winning paranormal and urban fantasy author, and also as Sophia Garrett, historical romance author. Her writing, however, skirted a fine line between hot and steamy, and motivated by authors she admired, she made the leap into sexier stories where the intimate relationship forges unbreakable ties.

Also by Tori St. Claire...

UNRAVEL ME

HER FORBIDDEN RISK

www.ingramcontent.com/pod-product-compliance
Lightning Source LLC
Chambersburg PA
CBHW020802250626
47155CB00003B/1175